A SCIENCE FICTION
ALIEN INVASION STORY

THE LORDS OF SUMMER

DOWNFALL

TRISTAN VICK

A REGOLITH PUBLICATIONS BOOK

THE LORDS OF SUMMER: DOWNFALL
Book 3 in The Lords of Summer Series
A Dark Forces of Nature Novella
By Tristan Vick ©2025. All Rights Reserved
www.tristanvick.com

Published by Regolith Publications
First Edition, copyright © November 24, 2025.

Stock Art "Meteor Shower" by: Andy_Art @ Pixabay
Final chapter art by: Christopher Awayan
Cover design by: Regolith Design
Written & Edited by Tristan Vick

ISBN: 9781950106189

Contents

1

DOWNFALL
PART 1: ONE WEEK LATER

Civilization didn't fall with a crash. It died with barely a whimper. A full week into the invasion, and most of the towns across the great American wasteland were deserted. People had been either evacuated or killed off by the hunter-killer aliens in the ensuing chaos. Almost overnight, the American landscape had turned into one giant ghost town.

After we'd watched Woodridge High School go up in flames, and with the town completely abandoned, we'd decided it was best to follow the only lead we had. Mr. Anders had told Jimmy "Mad Dog" Polson that my mom, Emily Mahoney, had been airlifted to Northwest Memorial Hospital in Chicago.

Since that was the only lead any of us had to go on, and since all of our parents had gone missing, most likely taken by the military to some secret base or bomb shelter somewhere, we'd decided to stick together and make the trek to Chicago, no matter what that entailed. So far, the only thing we needed to worry about was finding food and water.

For Billy, Jimmy, Paul, Mitch, and me, this summer had become the wildest summer of our lives. Alien invasion wasn't on our bucket list, but the aliens, it seemed, were just trying to survive.

Sarah's car ran out of gas in Dixon, Illinois, and all of the gas stations had been tapped dry, most likely by people leaving town or people hording gasoline as they prepped for the worse. But since Chicago was a hundred and three miles away, we decided to walk the rest of the way. At our current pace, Billy estimated that it would take us roughly five days to get to Chicago.

We raided a local sporting goods store, grabbed a couple of tents, some portable butane cooking stoves, a few sleeping bags, and hiking backpacks, water thermoses, flashlights, some cigarette lighters and anything else we could think of in terms of survival gear. Our only rule was you take what you can carry, because nobody else will carry it for you.

We camped out on the side of the highway, and hadn't come across so much as a single living soul. Heck, we hadn't even seen any of the thousands of aliens that had landed on earth, for that matter.

As far as we could tell, the meteor shower lasted for three whole days, and had brought with it tens of thousands of aliens, give or take. Due to the spotty news coverage over the past few days, and then the country-wide blackout, the exact number was uncertain.

Melody, being the math genius she was, estimated, based on the sheer number of meteor impacts, that it was closer to thirty thousand for the continental U.S., but that it might be two or three times that globally.

The majority of the aliens were Lucy's size—namely the size of a grizzly bear. However, some of the aliens were larger—being roughly the size of a large African rhinoceros.

"I'm tired of walking," Melody said. She paused briefly and threw her hands on her hips, taking a deep breath. "All we do is walk, walk, walk. It's sooo boring."

"I know it's boring," I said, nodding in agreement.

"But if we keep stopping, it'll take twice as long to get there."

"I'm fine with that," Jimmy said. "My feet are killing me. A more leisurely pace would be much appreciated."

I looked over at Billy who merely shrugged. I turned to Sarah and Megan when Megan said, "Taking a break sounds good, because I gotta piss like a racehorse."

Without so much as a warning, she walked off onto the shoulder of the road and pulled down her pants, squatted, and began to pee.

Jimmy's eyes grew three times bigger than normal and I quickly grabbed him by the arm and turned him away from her.

"I didn't see anything," Jimmy said.

"It's fine," I said. "I'm not worried."

"Oh, thank goodness," Jimmy replied, letting out a relieved sigh. "Because I saw a good solid butt cheek. But nothing else. I swear!"

I shot him a stern look but he was too busy fishing something out of his bag to notice. When I looked back toward Billy he was taking a drink out of his thermos. He emptied it and looked up into the container, hoping for one final drop.

Looking back at us, he said, "I'm all out of water."

"Me too," Jimmy said, opening a canteen and holding it upside down. Barely two drops drizzled out and he even patted the container trying to get another drop out.

"Billy is right," Sarah said. "There was a farm house a mile back down the road. I vote we head back and restock our supplies. Maybe bed there for the night."

Megan finished her business, stood up, buttoned her jean-shorts, and brushed the back of her shorts down to chase out any unwanted wrinkles. She also gave a quick tug on her jeans frayed edges to stop them from riding up and then looked up at us. We were all watching her.

Her cheeks turned slightly pink, from a twinge of embarrassment and she let out a nervous laugh. "Sorry about that, I really couldn't hold it."

"No, it's not that," I said.

"We're waiting to hear your opinion on heading back to the farmhouse," Sarah said.

"Oh," Megan laughed. "Sure. Why not?"

"You're in a cheerful mood," I said, nudging Megs

with my shoulders. She smiled at me.

"I feel so much better now. It's like a weight has been lifted."

"A weight has been lifted," I teased. "Two gallons back that away." I thumbed over my shoulder in the direction she'd taken a pee and she merely squinted at me with her piercing blue eyes.

"I don't know about you, Travis Mahoney. I think maybe you have a devious streak you're keeping secret from me."

"Nope," I said, smiling at her. "I am but a simple and humble boyfriend."

Megan's eyes widened as she stared at me. "So, we're boyfriend and girlfriend now, are we?"

I stopped in my tracks. "Well, I thought, because, you know, we… um… all the kissing and everything and… I mean… aren't we, well…?"

"Very eloquent," Melody quipped, rolling her eyes at my blubbering attempt to form a sentence.

Megan laughed and then grabbed me by my shoulders, looked into my eyes, and reeled me in for a hug.

With my face mashed into her chest, which I felt was probably deliberate, she replied, "Yeah, we are. I just hadn't labeled it yet. But I'm more than happy to call you my boyfriend, Travis "Maverick" Mahoney."

It was almost impossible for me not to blush. "Oh, I, uh, didn't know you knew my nickname."

"Know about your nickname or how you got it?" she asked, hinting at the fact that she knew the truth behind my nom de guerre. She laughed again and then relinquished the bearhug she had on me.

I rubbed my face, still in awe at where it had just been, and Megs punched me in the arm so hard it caused me to stagger back a few steps. As I watched her walk away from me, the sway and tilt of her hips moving seductively, Jimmy eased up beside me and let out an extra-long sigh.

"Remind me how you scored Megan McIntyre again?" We watched her walk away, both of our heads tilting to the right as we took in the view.

"I honestly couldn't tell you man. Probably a miracle."

My sis, Melody, spun around and, a mischievous gleam in her eye, quipped, "Oh, it was most definitely a miracle. In fact, it's such a gigantic miracle that it's veritable proof that God exists. There's really no other explanation for it."

She then pulled on her eyelid with her pointer finger, flashing the pink of her inner-eye, and then stuck her tongue out at us.

Megan laughed again, skipped up to my sister, and threw her arm around her and Sarah's shoulders. They all laughed and swayed up the street, all linked together as one girl-group.

Realizing that Billy had been quite for far too long, I spun around to see him standing about fifteen yards off. "Hey, Billy," I said. "What's up?"

Billy turned back toward Jimmy and me and shook his head. "It's probably nothing."

"What?" Jimmy asked, jogging up to him. "Did you see something?"

"I thought I saw something moving along the ridge of that hill over there." He pointed out at a cornfield and we both looked over at it. "About a quarter mile that way."

All three of us stood staring in the general direction, but there was no signs of movement.

"Should one of us go take a look," asked Jimmy. He brushed a hand through his flaming orange hair and then looked at Billy and I. "You know, just to be safe."

"It's probably nothing," Billy said.

"What if it's one of the aliens," I asked. "If it catches our scent, we might be in for a fight."

"I can go, if you want me to," Jimmy said.

"No," Billy said, shaking his head. "It's better if we stick together. If it is a hunter-killer alien, we'll cross that bridge when we come to it."

Jimmy nodded and he and Billy turned up the street and jogged to catch up to the girls.

I stayed back and stared long and hard. Of the group, Billy was the only one with 20/20 vision. And, I trusted his instincts. After all, he didn't get the nickname Billy "Backwoods" Bardem for nothing. He was a crack shot with a hunting rifle and if he really did see something, then I knew something was probably out there.

I held back and kept watching, because I was sure I'd see it too. It only took about a minute and then I saw it.

Although it wasn't an alien, Billy wasn't wrong, there was something definitely out there in the corn field. A small shadow moved along the horizon, just as he had said. But it was too small to be an alien. It was even too small to be a human, to my great relief. But it was fast. Real fast. And it was moving toward us.

That's when it burst through the wall of corn and I saw it. "Guys! Wait up," I hollered.

Everyone stopped where they were and spun around. "What is it Trav?"

I turned toward them and pointed over my shoulder. "Billy is right. There is something out there."

"Well," Melody said. "What is it?"

I turned back toward the field, put my fingers to my mouth, and whistled a high pitch whistle that could be heard in every direction. "Here boy!" I shouted. "Come here!"

Soon enough, making a B-line toward us was the happiest looking golden lab you'd ever seen.

I knelt down to be less intimidating and the dog ran up to me and leaped up, put its paws on my shoulders, and began licking my face.

"That's enough, boy," I laughed, turning my face away from the happiest dog kisses I'd ever received. "That's a good boy," I said in my baby-talk voice reserved for small children and puppies.

I patted the dog and then grabbed the tags dangling from his…erm… her collar. "Sif," I said aloud. I turned toward everyone who were now walking back to come see the dog. "Her name is Sif."

"What a perfect name for you, pretty girl," Melody said, crouching down beside me and scratching Sif behind her ears.

"I don't get it," Jimmy said.

"Sif is the goddess of the harvest and Thor's wife," I informed. "She's known for having golden locks of hair, just like the wheat fields."

"And she just happens to be a golden lab who came to us out of a golden corn field. Very fitting name," Megan said, leaning over and getting a few pats in.

"Can we keep her?" asked Melody, looking up at me and Megs and then turning toward Sarah. As our ex-babysitter, Melody still looked to her as a person of authority. Which made logical sense.

"I don't see why not," Sarah said.

"Great!" Melody replied, cheerfully jumping up. Sif hopped about as Melody played with her and I laughed. Standing up, I dusted off my hands and said, "All right, you two. We'd best get a move on."

"We've got a dog," Melody said, skipping up the street cheerfully. Safi was trotting happily behind her as she went. "We've got a dog!"

We all turned and followed after Melody and headed for that farmhouse we had seen up the road.

2

DOWNFALL
PART 2: FARMHOUSE

ONCE WE'D ARRIVED AT THE FARMHOUSE, WE gathered at the base of the front porch, which had a porch swing to one side, and stared anxiously at the door. It didn't look occupied, but we still needed to be sure. Sarah looked over her shoulder at us and said, "Stay here, y'all. I'll go knock. See if anyone is home."

Sarah walked up the short flight of stairs, the white painted wood panels creaking under each step, and cautiously moved toward the door. Slowly, she reached out, paused briefly to look back at us one last time, then knocked on the door. "Hello? Anyone home?"

She jiggled the handle but the door was locked from the inside.

"I'll go check around back," Jimmy said, racing off.

I raised my hand to caution him to wait, but he

was already rounding the bend at the other end of the house. Putting my hand down I turned to Billy and shrugged. "If he runs smack dab into an alien," I said. "That's on him."

"I wouldn't worry too much about Jimmy 'Mad Dog' Polson," Billy replied. "He can take care of himself."

A few more moments went by and then we all heard the sound of the door being unlatched from the other side and all turned towards the main entrance. The door swung open and Jimmy stood in the front entrance, freckles and all.

"It's empty," he said, throwing a thumb over his shoulder. "I mean, I didn't check upstairs yet, but I don't think anybody's home."

Billy was the first to enter and he said, "Jimmy, you're with me. We'll check out the upstairs."

Sarah followed him and said, "I'll check the kitchen and do a quick inventory."

"I'll help!" Melody said, hopping across the threshold, Sif prancing along after her.

I turned to Megan who merely looked at me with a strange expression on her face. She bit her bottom lip and almost looked, well, hungry for the lack of a better word for it.

"I saw a barn around back. Do you want to check it out with me? See if there's any tools, animals, or what not?"

"Sure," I said. Being inexperienced as I was, I'm a little ashamed to admit that I had not picked up on any of her signals. Not a single one.

Once we stepped inside the barn, to my surprise, Megs grabbed me, shoved me against the wall, and pressed her lips into mine.

We shared a lingering kiss and she moved into me, pressing her body against mine. She began kissing my neck and I grew nervous and gulped.

"What's going on here?" I asked.

"I'm kissing my boyfriend," she replied.

"I can see that," I laughed. Before things could get too heated, however, Melody's head poked in through the opening of the barn doors and she looked around for us.

"You guys! You've got to come see this!"

We followed her outside and then around the corner of the farmhouse. Out on the back patio was a hot tub. Jimmy already had it open and both Sarah and Billy stepped out of the back sliding glass doors just as

Megs and I arrived.

"Hey, guys," Billy said enthusiastically. "This house runs on propane gas and has a gas generator. And the toilets are on a septic tank. Heat still works. Power still works. Toilets still work. Everything still works."

"Talk about living off-grid," I said.

"Also," Jimmy said, hitting a switch. Bubble instantly began to churn and froth and the hot tub grew foamy white, "this hot tub still works."

"You were saying something about a bath?" Megs said, looking over at me.

We all needed to bathe desperately. But, if six of us took turns taking showers, there wouldn't be enough hot water. And assuming everyone only took a fifteen minute shower, that would still be ninety-minutes of bathing time.

Jumping into the jacuzzi, on the other hand, would kill two birds with one stone. We'd get clean and save time doing it. Not to mention everyone could enjoy the hot water and nobody would get stuck having to take a cold shower.

"I want to jump in sooo badly," Melody said. "But I didn't bring my swimsuit."

"None of us did," Sarah replied. She looked at everyone, and then, making the bold move, stripped down to her underwear, and climbed in.

"Well, heck, you don't gotta tell me twice," Jimmy said, overly excited by the prospect, and he stumbled over his own feet as he stripped to his boxers. He hopped in with a splash and everyone shielded their eyes.

Megs looked at me and not wasting another second, untied her jersey that hung around her waist, letting it fall to the ground. Next, she unfastened her jean shorts, peeled them off, revealing the black cotton panties she wore beneath, and climbed into the tub.

"All right, fine," I said. I also stripped down to my boxers and got in, sitting next to Megs. Billy did the same and we all looked over at Melody who stood by the back entrance, hemming and hawing.

Unable to make up her mind of whether she was going to get in, she held back and deliberated the pros and cons of having to strip down in front of everyone.

"Don't worry, Mel," I said. "There's just as much fabric in your underwear as a swimsuit. You'll be fine."

She bit her bottom lip and her eyebrows furrowed in consternation as she debated whether to get in. Deciding she didn't want to be left out, she looked up at us, and said, "All right, but nobody look till I get in."

She immediately began to strip down and we all turned away, giving her privacy to undress. After about thirty seconds, we heard a splash followed by a meager voice. "Okay, it's all right to look now."

"See, that wasn't so bad," I said.

She crossed her arms over her chest and said, "Shut up, you idiot."

"What are you afraid of," asked Jimmy. "It's not like we're naked or anything. Think of it like this, we're still wearing half of our clothes."

"It's not that," she said. "It's just…" She waded over to Megan and then cupped a hand to Megan's ear and whispered something.

"Oh, I see," Megan said. She then gave Melody a big hug. "That's perfectly normal. And, you don't need to worry. Sarah and I can answer any questions you might have."

"What kind of questions," Jimmy enquired. Billy and I shook our heads, warning him that he didn't want to know the answer to that. He merely scanned all our faces, noticing we were all leaning on him to drop it, and he asked, "What'd I say?"

"It's nothing I said," looking out at the field. "I'll explain it to you later."

"Fine," Jimmy said, folding his arms and pouting. "Keep your secrets."

"It's not a secret," Megan said. "It's a personal matter."

"Oh, like she has to poop, or something?" he asked, boorishly. Not having any sisters, or a girlfriend, Jimmy just didn't get it.

"My period, you dill-hole!" Melody shouted. "I'm talking about getting my period. Happy now?"

"Oh," Jimmy said, looking down at the water, growing bashful for perhaps the first time ever. He moved some bubbles around and then said, "I'm sorry. I didn't realize."

Sara gently touched Melody's shoulder and drew her over to her side of the hot tub. "It's okay. All women experience it. And Megan and I will help you in every way we can."

"I just didn't want to bleed in the tub and gross everyone out."

"You don't need to worry about that," Megan said. "You can swim in the ocean and sharks won't even know. Besides, it's not gross. It's beautiful."

"Well, maybe a little bit gross," Jimmy said without looking back up.

"Then, maybe you should know I'm on my period too," Megan said, her eyes drilling into the side of Jimmy's head.

"Me too," Sarah added. All three girls stared at Jimmy with intense gazes until he became noticeably uncomfortable.

"We're all bleeding right now. In fact," Megan added, "I'm actually surprised this whole jacuzzi doesn't overflow with our thick, red blood. I'm talking the parting of the elevator doors at the Overlook Hotel moment."

"Was that a *Shining* reference?" I asked.

"You better believe it," Megan said, proud of herself. She crossed her arms under her chest and gave Jimmy the ole evil-eye.

"Sorry, guys. But I'm outta' here," he said, springing up. "I can't be bathing in your girlfriend's bodily juices. It's just… wrong." With a splash, he hopped out of the jacuzzi, snatched up his clothes, and then disappeared inside the house.

Megan and Sarah just laughed.

"What?" I asked.

"I'm not on my period," Sarah said.

"Neither am I," Megan added. "We just wanted to mess with him."

"That's hilarious," Melody snickered.

"Be nice," I said. "The poor guy wants a girlfriend so badly. Meanwhile, it's the end of the world and we actually have women who are into us. I can see how that's a sore spot for him." I looked back toward the house.

"Sometimes, you're too nice," Melody said.

"That's one of the many things I like about you, Trav," Megan said, sliding up to me in the hot tub. "You're very compassionate. You truly care about others."

"I mean, I try."

"What about you, Sarah?" Melody asked. She looked right into Sarah's eyes and asked, "What do you like about Billy?"

"I, uh, well..." Sarah hemmed and hawed, and looked around at us all before turning back to Billy who was, in turn, waiting patiently for what she had to say. Instead, however, she got frustrated and then, stood up. "I think it's time for me to get out. I feel light headed. The hot water must be getting to me."

Billy stood up and touched her elbow. "Do you need me to come with you?"

"No," she replied. "I'm fine. Really. You stay. Relax. I'll scrounge up something for us all to eat."

She got out and Billy sat back down.

After Sarah left, he looked at Megs.

"Don't look at me, kid," Megan said. "She hasn't told me bupkis."

"It just seems like, I don't know, maybe she's having second thoughts about us. About me."

"Well, then," I said, splashing water into Billy's face. "Go and talk to her, you fool."

He looked at Megs, then me again.

"Yeah," Megan said. "Give her another minute to gather her thoughts, then go and talk to her. Don't leave unresolved stuff hanging only for you both to stew over. You'll only torture yourself with all the bad things you can think up and it might not be what she's thinking. So, just talk to her."

"All right. I will," Billy said, getting out of the tub.

After Billy left, I turned toward Megan and, without taking my eyes off of her, I said, "Mel, you may want to go inside too."

"But why?" Melody pouted. "I like it out here."

When she turned around, Megan and I were already sucking each other's faces.

"Ew! You guys!" Melody said, standing straight up. She was grossed out by our openly brazen public display of affection. "It's too much!"

She continued complaining as she climbed out of the tub and got her things. Her little wet feet clapped against the concrete of the back porch as she went inside, still complaining all the way into the house.

"Seriously. It's, like, all the friggin' time. You're going to dehydrate yourselves, get chapped lips, or worse. I'm telling you guys, this amount of sucking face isn't normal! I mean, do you even know what oxygen tastes like?"

Mel's voice trailed off as she muttered more complaints under her breath, most of which I ignored. Mel disappeared out of sight, and I turned and looked into Megan McIntyre's ocean blue eyes. Taking a deep breath, I slowly breathed out and then said, "I think I might be in love with you, Megan Michelle McIntyre."

"You think?" she asked with a laugh.

"I know," I replied.

"Good," she answered. "Also, I'm impressed that

you remembered my middle name."

"Yeah," I said. "I remember your mom yelling at you to stop hogging the bathroom on my third sleep over."

"And you've never forgotten it?"

"How could I?" I asked. "I was in love with you from the first time I saw you. I know it sounds cliché, like a bad romance movie. But it's true."

"Wow. It's so strange," she said leaning back. "That we felt this way about each other so early on."

"Maybe it's destiny," I said.

"Maybe." She nodded and then looked out at the sunset. "Maybe."

After a long silence of enjoying the sunset together, I asked, "Should we go find the others?"

"I suppose," she replied. There was definitely a reluctance in her voice. The moment was practically perfect and neither of us wanted to end it.

As nice as the moment was, though, dusk brought with her a sleepy shroud and one of my yawns triggered Megan to yawn too and we both realized it was time to call it a night.

3

DOWNFALL
PART 3: PERILOUS HIGHWAY

WHEN I ENTERED THE HOUSE, MEGAN HAD Jimmy pinned against the wall in the corner of the kitchen. She was still in her underwear, her wet hair dripping onto the linoleum floor. She held an arm up against the wall, blocking him in, her other arm pressed firmly against his throat.

"Repeat after me, dickface," she urged him. "Menstrual cycles are a normal part of female anatomy. Without periods, women couldn't have babies. Without babies, dipshits like me couldn't exist."

As I passed by, Jimmy mouthed the words, "Travis, help me!"

I grinned and continued on my way.

"Eyes up here," Megan said, grabbing Jimmy's chin and pulling his gaze back toward her. He gulped nervously.

"Do I have to?"

"Do you want to keep your manhood intact?" she asked. She then slapped the wall next to his head, startling him. "Then, say it!"

"Menstrual cycles are a normal part of the female anatomy without periods women couldn't have babies and without babies, dipshits like me couldn't exist."

"All in one breath," Megan said. "Impressive."

Jimmy ducked under her arm and then said, "I think, uh, I'm just going to go now. Sorry for the comments about your hot bod."

"Come here you little squirt!" Megan growled, and she chased after Jimmy who screamed like a girl as he ran for his life.

Melody laughed so hard she began to snort and her face turned so red I thought she might pass out. At the same time, Sif, our new golden lab, casually hopped onto the sofa and curled up to go to sleep.

Adding to the commotion, Sarah and Billy argued in the kitchen as they boiled hot dogs for dinner that we'd found in the freezer.

We kept only the living room lamp on, and drew all the curtains, so as not to attract any unwanted guests during the night. The last thing we needed was an alien invasion in the middle of the night while we slept.

Luckily, I was pretty sure that Sif would be able to alert us to any unnatural sounds coming from outside. If she began to growl or bark in the middle of the night, we'd jump up faster than a Mexican jumping bean.

The awkward part, though, was going through dinner with Sarah and Billy not talking to one another. They didn't say a single word the entire meal. Not to each other, not to any of us, they simply ate in silence and then got their sleeping bags out and set up camp on the opposite sides of the living room.

We had found three bedrooms upstairs, but one was made into an office and the other two looked slept in. None of us wanted to sleep in someone else's bed. Not with their smell still lingering in the house. It was strange.

Besides, we were all accustomed to sleeping together, as a close-knit group. As a clan. So, we all opted to camp out in the living room together.

As bedtime rolled around, Megan sat with Sarah talking on the opposite side of the room, Melody curled up with Sif on the sofa, and Billy, Jimmy, and I slept on the other side of the living room, near the opening to the kitchen.

"Hey," I asked, "Is everything okay with you two?"

Billy looked over at Sarah and then back at me. "I guess she's having second thoughts. Everything she'd warned Megan about, it turns out, she was feeling herself with me."

"Oh," I said. "Talk about feeling dejected."

"Rejection always hurts," Jimmy added.

"I said 'dejected'," I corrected.

"What?" asked Jimmy, shooting me a confused look.

"Nothing, man. Never mind."

"I think she was just missing her ex and needed someone to fill that void for a while. I suppose I should be glad she chose me… even if it was short lived."

"Hey, maybe she'll change her mind," Jimmy said.

"Nah, man. I'm fairly certain it's over. But it was fun while it lasted."

"You at least got to see her naked, right?" Jimmy looked to me and then Billy again. "I mean, I can't be the only one who saw her breasts. That wouldn't be fair, man. Not to you."

Billy shrugged. "Honestly, it wasn't that big of a deal to me. She's beautiful, and I wouldn't say no to seeing them. But as far as I know, she's only shown them to you."

"Well, that sucks," Jimmy said with a sigh.

Billy shrugged again. Then, Jimmy looked right at me, an unnerving smile forming on his face.

"What?" I asked, wondering why on Earth he was staring at me like that.

"Well, that's something you have to look forward to with Megan," he said.

"Not really," I replied. Both Billy and Jimmy shot me a confused look. "I've already seen Megan's breasts," I clarified.

"What?" Jimmy asked. "When did this happen?"

"He walked in on me in the shower," Megan informed us from across the room, signaling that they could hear everything we were talking about. "But it was totally an accident. Sometimes, I like to air-dry and, well, I guess I'd forgotten to lock the door that day."

"Yeah, right," Jimmy laughed, hitting me in the shoulder. "An accident." His sarcasm was palpable. "Also, it doesn't count because you were just kids then."

"No, no," Megan replied. "This was," she paused, tapping her chin as she tried to recall the exact date. "What was it, Trav? A couple weeks ago?"

"A couple weeks ago?!" Jimmy let out an audible gasp. "And you didn't tell any of us?!"

"Believe me," I said, "I wanted to tell you guys. I wanted to tell the entire world."

"So, what kept you?"

"I threatened to crush his nuts, tear them off, and feed them to him if he so much as mentioned my boobs to anyone."

"Yeah, that," I said.

Jimmy leaned in and whispered, "Is she always this scary?"

"Oh, I don't know," I replied, looking over at Megan who smiled and waved at me with her fingers. "She's mainly just super sweet all the time."

"I don't know," Jimmy said. "She talks a lot about ball-busting. And being the league champion for roller derby defenders, where they literally bust in each other's faces all night long, I'm inclined to take her word for it."

"Sure," I nodded in agreement. "She can be scary,

I guess. But she is also pretty damn awesome," I said, dreamily, still staring at Megan across the room. She blew me a kiss and I pretended to catch it.

Jimmy grabbed my hand and pried my fingers open, grabbed the imaginary kiss and pretended to throw it on the ground. "No," he said. "I won't tolerate any of that lovey-dovey crap."

I winked at Megs and then laid down onto my sleeping bag and rolled onto my side.

"I'm watching you two," Jimmy said, pointing at his eyes and then at both of us. "Like a hawk."

"Good to know," I said through a yawn. Lying across from me was Billy. He didn't say anything but his eyes were open and he stared right at me.

"I'm sorry," I said.

"Sorry for what?"

"That it didn't work out with you two."

"Everything has its time," he said.

"Very wise," I teased.

Billy smiled at me, kind of, and then rolled over so his back was facing me. With that, Jimmy reached up and turned off the lamp.

We all slept through the night without a hitch and when morning came we heard the cry of a rooster.

Jimmy sat straight up and said, "Did anyone else know there was a rooster on this farm?"

"Most farms," Megan said, sitting up and stretching her arms over her head as she fought through a long yawn, "have roosters."

"Oh, snap!" Jimmy said, jumping to his feet. "If there's a rooster, then there's chickens."

Jimmy shot out of the living room, through the kitchen, and out the back door. The commotion, along with the screen door slamming shut, roused us all awake and we slowly got out of bed. A few minutes later, Jimmy returned with an arm full of eggs.

"Breakfast anyone?"

"Did you see any pigs out there?" Megs asked.

"No," Jimmy replied. "Why?"

"Because, we could have had bacon too."

"That's horrible!" Melody said, rising to her feet.

Sif ran to the door and let out a low sounding woof. I walked over to her. "What is it, girl? Do you need out to pee?" I opened the door and Sif trotted out into the yard and squatted. When she was done, she began sniffing the ground and trotted off as she went to inspect the perimeter of the farm. I shrugged and let the door close.

After having eggs and toast, which we fried with butter on a big frying pan, we packed up our things and hit the road.

"Did I say how much I hate walking," Melody asked.

"*YES!*" we all said, simultaneously, letting her know the constant reminders were starting to get annoying.

When we came to the end of the drive, we heard a gentle bark and turned to find Sif running after us. Once she'd caught up to us, she slowed to a trot and kept our pace.

Billy and Sarah walked next to each other but they didn't speak. Megan and I held hands and Jimmy found a stick which he twirled about as though he were practicing slaying dragons.

"How much longer do you think it'll take us?" Melody asked, her brown eyes fixing themselves to me.

"Oh, I don't know," I replied. "If I had to guess, I'd say maybe three days."

"Three days of walking?" she griped.

"There's a big box store in the next town over… in about thirty miles…" Sarah informed us. "We can stop by there and restock on supplies, if it hasn't been completely raided yet."

We nodded and continued up the road for another couple of miles when we heard the roar of a V8 engine and the discharge of firearms.

"Everyone, get to the shoulder of the road and duck down in the grass," Billy shouted.

I tossed my backpack into the grass, helped Melody get hers off, and we all ducked down. Billy grabbed Sif and laid her on her side and stroked her gently to help calm her. Sarah and Megan slid down into the grass next to me.

Jimmy, however, was still standing in the middle of the street, curious to see what it was. "It's getting closer," he said.

"We know it's getting closer," I said. "Just get down."

Jimmy waited another couple of seconds then dove into the grass and waited. As the rumble of the engine grew louder and louder, more gunshots rang out. We all peered through the tall grass to see a burgundy Chevy K10, with a four-inch lift and BF Goodrich mud-terrain tires with maximum tread, zoom by us.

The driver revved the engine while his friend hung out the side of the passenger window and two other guys rode in the back. The two in the back wore cowboy hats and brandished matching machine guns which they fired intermittently into the sky.

As the truck passed us, and we could see into the back of the truck bed, we noticed that they'd killed an alien, its corpse strapped down in the back. This din of hooting and shooting was some kind of post-kill celebration, it seemed.

The men in the back of the pickup truck continued to whoop it up as they tore down the highway, and the guy in the passenger seat hung out of the side window and fired off a revolver, shouting, "Yee-ha!"

Obnoxiously noisy, the Chevy's V8 revved and growled all the way up the highway as the men continued to shoot their guns like a bunch of rednecks before disappearing around the bend a mile and a half down the road.

After they were long gone, we slowly emerged from the grass. Cautiously, we all gathered at the yellow dotted line in the center of the road and watched in every direction, still on high alert in case there were signs of other threats.

"That's what we have to be afraid of," Jimmy said. "My dad had friends like that. If you could even call them friends. They were always drunk. Would shoot their guns recklessly… sometimes inside the house… and they'd want to fight for no other reason than they got off on seeing others get hurt. But if you ever run into someone like that, you run." He turned to Melody and added. "You run and you hide."

"Hey," Megan said, stepping up to him. "You're scaring her."

"He's right, though," Billy said. "I remember this one time when Marvin and I stopped for gas on the way home from a hunting trip. A truck, not so unlike that one, pulled up alongside of us. They asked us about the buck strapped down to Marv's pickup bed, and commented on what a nice rack it had. We said thanks, thinking nothing of it, just a bunch of men being impressed by men stuff. But, then, four guys got out and opened Marv's truck and began to try and steal the buck we'd killed."

"What happened after that?" Sarah asked. It was the first time she and Billy had said anything to one another in the past eight hours. Which was weird, to say the least.

"Well, Marv grabbed the rifle off the rack in the back of the pickup and told them to get lost. They laughed at him and drew out their pistols. They were all packing. Every single one of them. I told Marv it wasn't worth getting killed over. So, we ended up letting them take it, antlers and all."

"That blows," Jimmy said.

"It wasn't all bad, though," Billy said, adding one last detail. "After our pit stop, we got back on the road and a couple miles out of town we saw that they'd been pulled over and were being ticketed for not having a hunting license. Marv and I flipped them the bird as we passed by and they couldn't do jack squat about it with a patrol car and two police officers breathing down their necks."

"Finally, some good news," Jimmy stated.

"What's so good about killing an animal?" asked Melody.

"Nothing," Billy said, redirecting her angry gaze from Jimmy toward him. "But Jimmy isn't wrong. If any of you guys ever run into people like that, you stay on guard. They only care about what they can get from you and how they can use you. And for the women, that might not be such a happy prospect."

"If anything," I interjected, "we need to continue to keep a low profile. Continue to stick together. And keep our eyes peeled... for aliens and road bandits alike. In times like this, people act crazy and make bad choices."

Just then we heard a clap of thunder and looked up at the sky. A stormfront with dark clouds and a navy blue sky pregnant with rain was fast approaching us. Lightning flashed and a clap of thunder caused Sif to let out a worried whine.

"I'm with the dog, on this one. We need to find shelter, and fast," I said.

"Should we head back to the farmhouse?" asked Melody.

"No, sweetie," Sarah answered. "It's too far now."

"It's about fifteen miles back that away," Billy said, pointing down the highway. "Straight into the eye of the storm."

"Wait, guys," Jimmy said. "I think I see something."

"What is it?" I asked.

"Over in that field. An old rusted out bus."

"I guess that'll have to do," Billy said. "Come on!"

We made a mad dash across a random field toward an old rusted out bus. As we approached, the downpour started and we were all drenched through and through before finally arriving at our destination.

"The roof has holes in it," Melody observed as we all clamored inside.

"Just stay to the side that doesn't leak," I said. "You'll be fine."

We all huddled in the back corner of the old, dilapidated bus and waited for the storm to pass. All of us were tired from the journey and sat in silence, only for the pitter-patter sound of raindrops and the occasional clap of thunder.

4

DOWNFALL
PART 4: MAD SCIENCE

Half way to Chicago, the sky darkened and the rainstorm of the century poured down on us. Luckily, we managed to find temporary shelter, but the storm wasn't letting up and we felt trapped. It was only an hour or so before we grew stir crazy.

"I don't think I can take much more of this," Jimmy said, standing up and walking over to one of the open bus windows. He peered out into the storm and wrapped his hands around his arms and rubbed his shoulders for warmth.

"This might be the first time I agree with Carrot-Top over here," Melody informed us, "but I don't want to be stuck in here forever."

Megan laughed. "It won't be forever, kiddo."

"Carrot-Top?" Jimmy scoffed. "I prefer Flaming Love Machine." He laughed at his own joke but we all gave him blank stares. "Because I'm a love machine."

"Yeah, we got it," Sarah said.

"Out of curiosity," Melody asked. "Since you don't have a girlfriend… who does the Love Machine do all the lovin' with?"

"His left hand, mostly," Billy teased.

"Come on, now!" Jimmy protested. "It's not fair if you all gang up on me."

"You sort of did it to yourself," I laughed. "Mr. self-proclaimed Love Machine."

"Well, perhaps. But," he added, tapping his temple and looking right at Sarah Lewis, "I've got all the material I need for a good time right up here."

"Oh, God," Sarah sighed. She rolled her eyes and looked away. "I knew it was a mistake the moment I did it."

"Yeah," Billy chuckled. "But you probably saved Travis's life."

"I wouldn't have shot him," Jimmy said, growing a little defensive.

"But you did fire the gun," Melody pointed out. "If Travis hadn't grabbed it and forced it out of your hands, who knows where that shot would have hit."

"Okay, okay. I get it, nobody is a Jimmy Polson

fan."

Growing red in the face, Jimmy couldn't keep his cool any longer and smashed one of the windows and angrily exited the bus.

After everyone grew silent again, I turned to Megs. "Seriously though, how do you find out about how I got my nickname?"

"Mitch is my brother," she said, smiling coyly.

"Yeah, but on a blood pact, we swore secrecy. Nobody was ever to learn about that."

"Oh, now I have to know," Sarah said, leaning forward and wrapping her arms around her knees. She blinked at me innocently and then looked to her bestie for answers.

"Should I say?" Megan asked, looking back at me.

"I mean, I guess the cat is out of the bag, so, why not?"

Megan's eyes lit up as she got to tell her account of how I came to be called Travis "Maverick" Mahoney.

"So, as I understand it, it was in the sixth grade during one of Mrs. Parker's field trips."

"Oh, I remember her," Melody said. "She was super pretty."

"Right. And the guys all dared Travis here to do something bold. Something stupid to express his undying love for her."

I looked at everyone's confused expressions and raised my hands. "It's nothing weird, I swear. She was my first crush. That's all."

"Exactly," Megan continued. "And so they dared you to do what again?" Megan smiled at me and I shrugged. "They dared him to walk right up to her and kiss her on the lips."

"You kissed a teacher?" Melody gasped. "That's gross."

"He did," Jimmy said. "And he liked it."

"He also got slapped and sent back to the bus for the remainder of the field trip," Billy added. "But from that day forward, we knew this little daredevil would take any dare. He was the wild card of the bunch. Our very own little…"

"Maverick," Megan said, finishing Billy's sentence as she smiled at me.

"You do realize I think it's a little weird how excited you get by the fact that I kissed another woman."

Megan reached over and squished my cheeks

together with one hand. "It's so cute that you think that."

"I heard that Mrs. Parker got fired over that," Billy said. "Something about inappropriate conduct with a student."

"Oh, that wasn't me," I said.

"Are you sure?" Megan teased, as she kept my face squished in her fingers, clinging to me like an overly affectionate kitten.

"Pwetty-suuure," I spoke through forcefully pursed lips. Megs let go of me then playfully slapped my face.

"No, you're right," Megan informed. "It wasn't you. It was Dean…" she suddenly caught herself, realizing she wasn't supposed to divulge that sensitive information, especially considering that Dean was Sarah's ex. Everyone grew deathly quiet and the awkward moment took root.

Turning toward Sarah, she said, "I'm sorry. I wasn't thinking…"

Sarah shook her head. "It's no big deal. I think the whole town knew about that."

"I didn't know about that," I said.

"Will somebody please tell me what anyone is

talking about?" Melody said, feeling a bit peeved she wasn't able to follow what was going on.

"We'll tell you when you're older," I promised.

"Oh, great. So, now I get to imagine all these horrible scenarios in my mind, wondering if any of them are at all accurate depictions of reality."

"Isn't that all of us?" I asked.

"No," Billy said. "I'm pretty sure it's just you two."

"All right," Sarah said, standing up and brushing down her skirt. "Changing the subject, yeah? So, it looks like the next town is seven to ten miles down the road. If we can get there, we can maybe find some better shelter and a place to stay dry."

Sif, who was lying next to Melody sat up and barked.

We all looked toward the entrance of the bus and Jimmy popped into view. "You guys! Look what I found!" Jimmy reached into his jacket and pulled out a map.

"A map?" asked Melody

"Yes. A map!" he exclaimed, still excited by his unique discovery.

"What's so good about having a map?" Melody asked rhetorically. It was more of a statement, actually. "We already know this road goes straight into Chicago."

"Yeah, I know that," Jimmy replied. "But we didn't know all the stops or how far apart the towns were, till now!"

"I mean, I guess that could be useful," I said.

Jimmy spread the map out on the back of one of the chairs and then pointed at something. "But check this out."

"All I see is an empty field," Sarah said.

"Look closer," Jimmy said.

Sarah leaned in and took a closer look as asked. "The CDC?"

"Yeah. Center for Disease Control!"

"Great," I said dryly. "But what's so great about the CDC?"

"They'll have scientists there, right? Maybe one of them will know something about the aliens."

"You do realize the CDC is where they keep dangers diseases like smallpox and malaria, right?" Megan asked.

"Everyone knows that," Jimmy said, deflecting.

It was clear to anyone present that he didn't know what the CDC stood for, let alone what they did there.

He was just excited by the prospect of talking to a scientist and getting some answers.

"I don't want to catch any diseases," Melody said.

"You won't," Sarah said. "They keep them frozen, in special containers, inside sealed freezer vaults. You're actually less likely to get sick in their sterile labs than you are out here in the real world."

"Oh," Melody said, pondering the ramifications of deadly disease.

"Guys, I know it's a lot to ask, but we should at least check it out. It's on the way, so we don't have to detour more than a mile or two. And if there is a scientist there, we can maybe get some answers."

"I'm all for it, if you guys are," Billy said.

"It couldn't hurt," Megs said.

So, with that decided, we gathered our things and made the ten mile trek to the Center of Disease Control. When we got there, however, we immediately regretted our decision.

Dead bodies littered the entire parking lot.

"What in the seventh level of Hell happened here?" asked Jimmy.

We all stood at the edge of the parking area and looked at roughly a dozen dead bodies, some of them wearing lab coats.

"None of them look like they were attacked," Melody said.

Sif whined and turned a couple of tight circles before slowly backing away from the parking area.

"I think the dog might have the right idea," Billy said. That's when we heard a voice call out to us.

"Hey, you kids, it's not safe out there!" We looked at the main entrance to see a man in a white lab coat waving to us. "You need to come inside, get out of the rain."

We all looked at each other and other than the spooky fact that the whole place was surrounded by dead bodies, we really didn't want to stay in the rain.

Reluctantly, we all crossed the parking lot, all of us except for Sif, our golden lab, who stayed back, keeping a safe distance away from the scent of death and other terrible things that only a dog's heightened senses could detect.

As for the rest of us, we decided to risk it.

Having entered the facility, the scientist handed us towels and waited for us to dry off before introducing himself. "I'm Dr. Franklin Castle. But I'm not a medical doctor. I'm a geneticist. So, I can't heal any of you if you're hurt."

"I think we're fine," Billy added. The doctor nodded.

"What's a geneticist?" asked Jimmy as he ran a towel through his red hair.

Dr. Castle's face lit up. It was clear he hadn't had anybody to talk to in days and he was happy to educate us. "I look at the gene sequences in a living organism's DNA, including viruses and the like."

"DNA?" Jimmy asked, still oblivious.

"It's the stuff in your blood," Melody said. "It's what makes you human."

"That's right," Dr. Castle said. "This kid gets it. It's the genes in your DNA that make you uniquely human."

"So, like a dog's DNA would be different from our DNA?" Jimmy looked at all of us and then turned to Dr. Castle again.

"Correct. Every species has its own unique DNA. A human's DNA is different than a turtle's DNA which is different than a pigeon's DNA. But enough talk about DNA. I'm sure you kids are famished, so if you'll all follow me to the galley."

"This place has a galley?" Billy asked.

"What's a galley?" Melody enquired.

"It's like a big kitchen with a restaurant attached."

Melody nodded and we followed Dr. Castle to the galley and there was already food, not more than a day old, waiting for us.

"The open fridges have sandwiches, there's chili in the soup container, and there's pizza and fried chicken in the heated displays."

"Oh, my God," Megan said, her stomach growling. "I don't think I've ever been so grateful to see home-cooked food in my life."

"Grab yourself a plate and dish up. Help yourselves to as much as you can eat," said Dr. Castle.

We all dished up, every single one of our plates a heaping pile of food, and then went and sat together at one of the long tables. As we ate, I looked over at Dr. Castle who leaned on one of the salad bars and smiled at us.

"Are you having any?" I asked, mouth full of fried chicken.

"Oh, I already ate," the doctor replied.

Halfway through our meal, Sarah coughed a couple of times, but she kept eating. Another minute passed, and she coughed again. Then a whole fit overcame her and she stood up.

"Are you all right?" asked Billy, standing up and touching her back. "Are you choking?"

Sarah shook her head. "No," she wheezed. "Something else… is wrong… I… can't… breathe."

More coughing overtook her and Billy turned toward Dr. Castle.

"You've gotta do something."

"Interesting," the Doctor said.

"Interesting?" I asked. "What do you mean by that?"

Dr. Castle raced to the hallway, disappeared around the bend, then reappeared a moment later wheeling a gurney which he parked beside the table. "Quick, kids. Help me get her onto this."

Megan got under Sarah's arm and, with Billy's help, hoisted Sarah onto the mobile bed.

"Why do I get the feeling you know what's happening?" asked Megan, eyeing Dr. Castle with a hard as nails glare.

"Let me put it to you kids plainly, your friend has alien DNA inside her and she's rejecting the serum I dosed you all with."

Jimmy, who was mid bite through a chicken leg,

spit it out. "Wait, are you saying you poisoned the food?"

"I medicated the food," the doctor confessed. "And now your friend here is having an allergic reaction."

"Because of the alien DNA?" asked Melody.

"This one is bright, isn't she?" Dr. Castle smiled at Melody and then, pushing the gurney out into the hall, he said, "Follow me, kids. We've got to get your friend proper medical attention."

"I thought he said he wasn't a medical doctor," asked Jimmy looking at all of us.

I shrugged. "I don't know, man. But Sarah needs our help." I began running after Dr. Castle and Sarah and looked back to see the gang still frozen in their tracks. "Come on!" I shouted. That got them moving.

Dr. Castle wheeled Sarah into a large medical lab and put her under a large light. He then flipped a switch and the light turned ultraviolet and Sarah's veins glowed hot pink.

She groaned and twisted under the light.

Billy was the first to speak. "What's happening to her?"

"Her body is rejecting the serum. I designed it to

counteract the alien DNA. Once the aliens infect you, there DNA slowly begins to override your own. How long has she been infected for?"

"We didn't even know she was infected," Jimmy said.

"No, that's not entirely true," I said. "Remember? When we found her in the woods, she had lacerations all across her body from being attacked."

"Lucy didn't mean to hurt her," Melody said. "He was just scared."

"Lucy?" the Dr. asked.

"It's her pet alien," Megan said.

"Pet alien?" he asked, looking over at Melody.

"They're actually quite nice, if you feed them chocolate," Melody informed him.

"I have a million questions, but right now, we need to help your friend, otherwise she could end up like the others."

"What others?" asked Billy.

"I think you saw them, in the parking lot," Dr. Castle replied. "They had all been infected too. But by a much higher dose. If your friend was merely grazed, another dose of serum may cure her."

"Or kill her, you mean," Billy said.

"If we don't give her the serum, she will slowly die over the next week, perhaps two, as the alien's DNA rewrites hers. Eventually, she'll experience organ failure as her body goes haywire. Then she'll get a fever, hot sweats, chills, and eventually she'll bleed out of her eyes and ears as her cells burn out."

"Can you save her?" asked Megan. She spoke our minds and we all looked to Dr. Castle.

"I believe I can," he answered as he walked over to a refrigerated cabinet. It was a stainless steel fridge, and he opened it, pulled out a glass vile of turquoise liquid, and then prepped a fresh syringe. After getting it ready, he put the needle in the vile and sucked out the turquoise liquid.

"I'll need to inject her with this."

"And what, exactly, is that?" asked Jimmy.

"It's more serum," the Dr. replied, almost proud of himself in some kind of way. "It's a more highly concentrated dose than what you consumed in the food. But it will cure her."

"Could it kill her?" asked Billy. He reached down and took Sarah's hand in his.

"There is, I'm afraid, a small probability that her body will fully reject the serum and she might die, yes.

But that's not going to happen."

"How can you be sure?"

"Because, I've tested it thoroughly," Dr. Castle replied.

Right then and there, it dawned on us what he meant. He'd tested it on the others. The poor souls who were laying in the parking lot outside of the science lab.

Billy got between Dr. Castle and Sarah, who gripped her sides and moaned out in pain. "What are you, like some kind of mad scientist or something?"

"You don't understand, kid. The aliens are taking over the world. Not by force. But discreetly, with their DNA!"

"Lucy would never do that!" Melody shouted.

"It burns," Sarah gasped between waves of pain.

"Come on," I said, grabbing the gurney. "We're getting out of here."

"No, wait," Dr. Castle said, raising a hand. "You'll only kill her if you take her away from here. She needs progressive treatments of serum so she can fight off the alien DNA that's seeped into her system."

"I don't think you're catching the hint," Megan said, cracking her neck as she rocked her head back and forth on her shoulders. "She's not staying here with you. We're taking my friend, and we're leaving."

"I'm afraid I can't let you do that," Dr. Castle said. "You'll only risk infecting others if you let her leave here."

I gave Megan the nod of approval and she nodded back. Then, using her full weight, she body-checked Dr. Castle into the cabinet. He definitely wasn't ready for getting hit let alone getting hit by the roller derby blocking queen, Megan "Powerhouse" McIntyre.

Glass shattered as Dr. Castle rebounded off the cabinets and collapsed to his knees. As he looked up, he growled, "You kids will regret this! I tried to warn you. But you've doomed us all!"

Megan flew forward with a flying knee kick, like in kickboxing, and in a single blow knocked Dr. Castle unconscious. He collapsed to the cold floor of the lab and lay there, dreaming of little birdies floating around his head.

"Nice one!" Jimmy said.

"Help me wheel her out," Billy said, pushing the gurney. As we began to head back toward the entrance, Megan was patting the doctor's body down.

"What are you doing?" I asked.

"This fool has to have some keys on him... ah, here we are." She stood up and jingled the keys in front of her.

"Smart," I said.

We ran into the parking lot and paused at the vast separation of cars.

"It'll take forever to find the right car," Melody said, letting out a disappointed sigh.

"It was a nice idea," I said. I touched Megan's arm and she drew back and then threw the keys halfway across the parking lot.

"At least I can force that dickwad to walk home," she said.

"What we need are wheels... like those," Jimmy said, pointing at something across the street.

On the opposite side of the street sat a bicycle shop with plenty of bikes. We ran up to the windows and pressed our faces against the glass as we looked at all the wonderful new bikes.

"Nice find," I said, slapping Jimmy on the back.

Relieved to find the front door unlocked, we stepped under the yawning and entered the shop. Splitting up, we each took an isle as we looked for our dream bikes.

As we browsed the store, Sarah was already starting to feel a little better and managed to stand on her own without help.

"How are you feeling?" Billy asked. His eyes looked worried, but he merely offered her support and reached out and touched the top of her hand.

"I feel like I got hit by a bus," she replied, pinching the bridge of her nose and squinting as though she had a nasty headache. "But, otherwise, I'm peachy."

"The good news is that you're alive," Megan said. "That's what matters."

"Thanks to all of you." Sarah placed a hand on my shoulder and then scanned everyone's faces. "There's no telling what would have happened if he'd pumped my body full of that stuff."

"I mean," Jimmy looked around at all of our faces, "it seemed pretty clear by the amount of bodies that were piling up in the parking lot what the end results of his experiment would be. That guy wasn't right in the head."

"You can say that again," I said, agreeing wholeheartedly with Jimmy's assessment of Dr. Castle. The good doctor wasn't good at all. He was a complete and utter crackpot.

"Look guys," Melody said. "The rain is letting up."

"Perfect timing," I said while Jimmy, Billy, and Megan grabbed mountain bikes. Melody grabbed a pink bike with a white banana seat and tassel handlebars.

As for me, I found a three-wheel rickshaw that would allow Sarah to ride as a passenger as I peddled.

Holding out my hand, I said, "Your chariot awaits, milady."

Sarah laughed. "Thank you, my liege," she replied, taking my hand and hopping on.

We pushed our bikes out to the street and then hopped on. As we peddled down the main street, we heard barking coming from up the road and looked back to find Sif, our faithful golden lab, running up to us and joining our excursion.

"Jimmy?" Sarah said, beckoning him over to us. He rode his bike over to us and looked at her curiously.

"Yeah?"

"From now on, no more pit stops."

"Right," he said.

Everyone had a good laugh and we continued up the road, passing a road sign along the way that said eighty-one miles to Chicago.

5

DOWNFALL
PART 5: ROAD WARRIORS

Nearly thirty miles down the road, we hit the brakes and our bike tires screeched as we skidded to a halt in the middle of the road. Parked directly in our path about two hundred meters from us was the burgundy Chevy pickup truck we'd seen earlier.

Two of the men leaned against the trucks as they held their rifles. In the back of the truck was their latest kill, covered by a blue tarp.

Billy and I shared glances and then we slowly peddled up to them.

"Stop there," one of the men said, stepping forward and raising a hand. "It's not safe up this way."

"But," I said, "we need to get to Chicago."

"He ain't heard, yet," the other man said.

"Heard what?" Jimmy asked.

"Chicago has been overrun by these vermin." The man reached back and pulled off the tarp, revealing the dead alien in the back of the pickup.

"Holy geez," Jimmy said. "You got one of them?"

We all knew it was an act. But Jimmy said his dad knew guys like this and was probably hamming it up to stroke their egos and get on their good side.

"Yeah," the first man, who wore a red and black plaid flannel shirt, answered. "It's our third kill this week."

"Rad," Jimmy replied, craning his neck to better inspect the dead alien.

"You wanna touch it?" the second man asked. He had on a blue denim shirt and a straw cowboy hat.

"I mean, under normal circumstances we would," I said. "But my mom is in Chicago. We have to keep pushing onward."

"You got a hearing problem?" the flannel man asked. "I said Chicago ain't open. We're setting up blockades all across the great state of Illinois to prevent people from entering the city."

"And who are you people, exactly?" asked Billy.

Both men turned toward Billy Bardem and looked at him with hardened gazes. Their eyes were cold, like glass marbles, and they gave up on any pretense of trying to be nice.

The flannel man spit and then said, "We're Illinois State Militia, son. You'd be wise to heed our advice. If we let you go on past, there's no telling what kind of harm my come your way. If you turn back now, though, you have our word that you and your little friends here will be safe."

"No place is safe," Melody said.

I shot her a look that relayed, with strong facial language, that now was not the time nor the place for her smarty-pants attitude.

The man in denim knelt down and, resting his rifle across his lap, smiled at Melody. "Well, little lady. That may be more or less true. But, you see, Chicago is especially unsafe. So, you're safer on this side of the line than that." He looked over his shoulder and then turned his intense, seemingly predatory gaze back to Melody who merely drew back a few steps.

The way he was looking at her unnerved us all. He smiled at her and kept on smiling. The smile never faded or melted. It was as if he wanted her to know he was nice. So, he kept on smiling, to the point where it felt unnatural. And then he smiled some more. Of course, the longer he smiled, the more tense his facial muscles grew and the more manic and frightening his smile became.

Seeing as Melody was frozen with fear, Megan rolled up beside Melody and reached over and placed a supportive hand on Mel's shoulder.

"All I meant was there's aliens everywhere," Mel stated, kicking a pebble as she straddled her bike seat.

The man in denim stood up and chuckled. "Well, yes. That seems to be the sad state of affairs we find ourselves in. Overrun by extraterrestrial rodents of unusual size."

"As we said," the flannel man interjected, getting back to the topic at hand. "You kids best turn right around and head back to wherever it is you came from."

"I'm sorry," I said, "But our town was completely destroyed. There's nothing to go back to."

"That's the pits," the denim man said, smiling at us all. He still gave an air of extra-politeness. The kind of politeness that Jehovah Witnesses or Mormon missionaries exhibited when meeting strangers. It was almost too nice. It was certainly suspect.

Meanwhile, while he smiled perhaps a little too

much for our tastes, the other man had a more hardened exterior and hardly smiled at all. He had that "tough guy" persona down pat.

"I don't mean to overstep," I said. "But we're willing to take the risk. There's just no place else for us to go."

The flannel man banged on the side of the truck and said, "Let them through, Vinny."

The truck roared to life, revved a couple of times, then slowly pulled over to the side of the road. The denim man merely gestured for us to freely pass on by. "Stay safe, kids."

"We will," Jimmy replied. He tapped his fingers to his forehead and gave them another two-finger salute, as a gesture of thanks.

As we rode on by, it felt a little weird as all eyes watched us. Gradually pulling away, Billy was the first to break the silence.

"Is it just me, or did that seem weird to anyone else?"

"Oh, it was definitely sweird," Megan agreed. "The way that one guy kept smiling at us. Especially Melody. It gave me the creeps."

"We're going to need to find a place to stay the

night," Jimmy said. "And preferably away from the road since I have a feeling those guys will be looking for us tonight."

"Jimmy," Sarah said, leaning forward and peeking out from the hood of the rickshaw, "I think it's time to get your map out and figure out a good place to rest for the night."

"You mean, like a… pitstop?" he asked, squinting at her.

She widened her eyes in exasperation and then conceded. "Yes, Jimmy, like a pitstop."

Jimmy skidded to a stop, got out his map, hopped into the rickshaw, and sat down beside Sarah Lewis. To our amusement, Sif hopped up to, and squeezed in between them as they inspected the map together.

After a while, Jimmy pointed at a location and said, "Here we go. This, right here."

"Malta?" asked Sarah. "Why Malta?"

"There's a Methodist church here," Jimmy replied.

"And how's that going to help us?"

"Because, those knot heads back there wouldn't think to look for us in a church. All we need to do is go ditch our bikes by someplace like a school or a police station and then hide in the church," Jimmy informed.

"It says it's only eleven miles down the road. We can do that before nightfall," Sarah added.

With the wind at our backs, we peddled furiously and did as Jimmy had suggested by stashing our bikes in the alley next to the police station.

To our pleasant surprise, the Methodist church also contained a dormitory. Which meant we all had beds to sleep in. And there were twelve rooms and six of us.

We just made sure to keep to the room opposite the street side, because, sure enough, midnight came, the gentle rumble of a V8 alerted us to the fact that the flannel and denim man, and whoever Vinny was, had followed us to the small town.

They drove up and down, tracing every street looking for us. We peeked out of the curtains and watched the headlights of the Chevy roaming up and down every street and alley, until finally it came to a halt near the police station.

"They found the bikes," whispered Billy.

I turned around and motioned for Sarah to come close. "We need to find places to hide, just in case they do decide to search the church."

Megan and Sarah located several good places to hide inside the church while Billy, Jimmy, and I secured all the windows and doors. Once everything was locked down tight, we returned to the third floor bedrooms.

"Guys," Melody whispered. "I think they're leaving."

We peaked out the windows and, sure enough, it was just as Melody had described. The Chevy's tail lights turned up the highway and slowly headed away from town, growing smaller and dimmer as they retreated into the night.

"I suppose the good news," I said, "is we can hear them coming from a mile away."

"All right, everyone," Sarah said. "Let's try our best to get some sleep. We have a long day tomorrow as we start the last leg of our journey."

Everyone returned to their rooms to turn in for the night, everyone but Megan, that is. Instead of finding her own room, she came to mine.

"Is it all right if I sleep with you?" she asked. "I mean, we don't need to do anything. I just want to cuddle."

"Sure," I said, opening the covers and letting her climb into my bed.

Simply due to her size, Megan was the big spoon by default. But, I really didn't mind. I liked being held. Especially when she pulled me into her warm, soft body.

We were dozing lightly, enjoying one another's warmth when Sif barged into my room, placed her front paws on the window sill and started growling lightly.

Megan and I got up and went over to the window. Gently pulling the curtain back, we leaned forward and peered outside. Standing in the middle of the street was the man in flannel. Moonlight painted him in highlights that let us see him, even in the dark. It still seemed like he could sense us, because he tipped his hat back and looked up at our exact window.

We both startled and stepped away from the windows. "Did he see us?" I asked.

"I don't think so," Megan said. We looked at each other and nodded. Building up the nerve to look outside again, I drew the curtain to the side and we looked out at where the flannel man had been standing, but he was gone.

"That's not creepy at all," I whispered.

"I'll go wake the others," Megan said. As she turned toward the entrance, Billy appeared from the hallway, crossbow in hand.

"You all stay here," he said. "I'll handle this."

"You sure you don't want any backup?" I asked.

"If I fail to get rid of the prick, he'll be coming for you guys next. You stick together and help each other." With that said, Billy disappeared into the darkened corridor.

Megan and I gently roused everyone from their sleep and found our designated hiding places.

Jimmy was the only one who didn't lock himself away into hiding, so when the gun shot went off, he was the first to boldly race down the stairs.

Naturally, we all grabbed our weapons and followed after him. When we arrived downstairs, lying in the dining room was Billy Bardem, gunshot wound to his shoulder. Lying opposite him, was the flannel man, a crossbow bolt sticking out of his left eye socket.

"You all right, Billy?" Jimmy asked, falling to his knees and sliding up to Billy, who merely held his shoulder and grit his teeth as he pushed down the pain.

"That S.O.B shot me," Billy said through clenched teeth.

"You're lucky he didn't kill you," Jimmy said.

As Jimmy attended to Billy, I went over to the man and checked his pulse. When Billy and Jimmy looked at me, I shook my head. He was dead.

"Shit," Billy said.

Megan arrived next and she helped Billy sit up. "Jimmy, turn on that light. Travis, get me some hot water."

"What can I do?" asked Melody. We turned to see her standing in the doorway. Sif stood next to her, wagging her tail and panting heavily.

"Find a first aid kit and some bandages or gauze. That sort of thing."

"I'm on it," she said. She passed Sarah in the doorway as she scurried to the first floor bathroom to look in the medicine cabinet.

Sarah just stood in the door looking at Billy, tears in her eyes. "What were you thinking, you big idiot?"

"I was protecting all of you."

"It looks like it went straight through," Megan said. She stuck her finger in Billy's wound and he groaned.

"What the Hell, Megan?" he griped.

"Sorry. Sorry," she said. Then, turning to me, she added, "It definitely went straight through."

"That's good news," Jimmy said. "We'll clean you up and stitch you up and you'll be as good as new."

"Not after I'm done with him, he won't," Sarah said.

We all looked at her and Billy just laughed.

"What's so funny Billy Marcus Bardem?"

"Oh, snap!" Jimmy said. "She knows your middle name."

"Nothing," Billy replied. "It's just that, for the past two days you haven't talked to me after telling me you weren't in love with me anymore and wanted to take time apart."

"And…?" she asked.

"And now, here you are crying over a flesh wound. So, which is it? Do you care for me or don't you?"

Billy looked right into Sarah's tearful eyes waiting for her answer.

"That's unfair," she said, angrily. "And you know it."

"Do I, though?" he asked.

"I found a first-aid kit," Melody chirped, returning to the kitchen.

I ran the tap water until it was piping hot and then doused the towel I'd found hanging next to the stove and handed it over to Megs.

She dabbed Billy's shoulder wound with the hot cloth and then, using the thread and needle from the first-aid kit, patched him up. Biting off the line, she then cover his stitches with a gauze pad and then a sticky pad.

"There," she said. "That ought to do it."

"Thanks," Billy said, looking right at Megan. "I owe you."

"You owe me nothing," Megan said, helping Billy to a chair next to the dining room table. "You've been shouldering the brunt of our burdens from the beginning, and you're just a kid."

Sarah marched over, grabbed Billy by the hand, and then towed him behind her. As they headed towards the stairs, she said, "By the end of tonight, he'll be a man."

Sarah practically dragged Billy upstairs and we all looked at one another in stunned silence.

Jimmy gulped and then asked, "Do you think she's actually going to… you know?"

"None of our business," I said.

"I like to imagine that they're just holding hands and telling each other secrets," Melody said.

"Yeah, that's exactly what they're doing," Jimmy fired back sarcastically.

Megan slapped Jimmy upside the back of his head and he yelped and rubbed his head.

"Mel, you take Sif and go back to bed. As for you two idiots, help me roll this body up in the dining room rug."

Melody nodded and did as requested, took Sif, and headed back to bed. Meanwhile Megan, Jimmy, and I rolled the flannel man into the rug. By the time we'd wrapped him up, he was snugger than a burrito.

Megan held the top half, I held the man's feet, and Jimmy held the middle. Slowly, we maneuvered through the kitchen of the church, took him out the back door, and carried him into the alley.

"What if his friends come looking for him?" asked Jimmy as we set the bundled up body down behind the trash cans.

"We'll be long gone before then," Megan said.

"We leave tonight," I added. "We can pick a random town along the road to sleep this afternoon. Until then, we get our bikes and ride like crazy to the next town."

"Screw that," Jimmy said. "I'm done biking."

Megan and I looked over at him and he was staring at a silver 1984 Mercedes-Benz 300 series parked in the driveway of a house across the street.

"Wait here," Jimmy said as he darted across the street. In another minute, he disappeared around the corner of the house and I looked over at Megan.

"I don't think we should leave him to his own devices. He's liable to hurt himself."

We jogged across the street but by the time we got to the curb the house's garage door began to open. The sectional garage door rattled as it rose up, and Jimmy stood on the other side, a big grin on his face. He held up the car keys, showing us his exceptional find.

"They were just hanging on the kitchen wall by the door to the garage. Easy-peasy, lemon squeezy," he said.

Jimmy walked over to the driver's side, opened the door and was about to get in when Megan grabbed his wrist. "Do you have a driver's license, Jimmy Polson?" she asked him.

"What is this, an interrogation?"

"Well, do you?"

"Uh, not exactly," he said.

"Then give me the keys."

"Ah, man," Jimmy sighed, reluctantly handing over the keys to the Mercedes. "Your girlfriend is a real buzz-kill, did you know that?"

I ignored Jimmy's comment and sat down next to Megan while Jimmy climbed into the back seat, so as not to cramp us up front. Megan put the key in the ignition, twisted it, and the engine sputtered to life.

"Woo!" she hooted, excited by the fact that she was able to get the car to start in one go.

Applying pressure to the gas, we were rolling in no time. Megan did a U-turn, so we ended up on the other side of the street. She pulled around the bend and parked the car beside the sidewalk, directly in front of the main entrance. Turning off the motor, she looked at us, and said, "Let's get the others. Then we'll drive to the next town over like we've discussed."

It only took us about fifteen minutes to gather our stuff, carry my sleeping sister down to the car, and pile in. Luckily, the Mercede's 300 class trunk was enormous and managed to fit all our gear. But the car ride was a tight squeeze because it was Megan, me, and Jimmy up front while Billy, Sarah, my sister, and Sif, our faithful golden lab, sat in back.

Because Sif was nearly the size of Melody, however, we'd jammed our sleeping bags behind the driver's seat to make a kind of bed for Melody and Sif to lay down on.

As Megan pulled away from the church, she turned off the headlights so that nobody could see what direction we were heading in the dark.

Jimmy sat up on his knees and twisted around to face the back. "So, did you guys do it?" he asked, wiggling his eyebrows at them and shooting them a sly smile.

"None of your bee's wax," Sarah said, grabbing Jimmy's face and spinning him back around. Jimmy plopped down next to me and crossed his arms, disappointed that he didn't get the nitty gritty details of whatever it was they'd gotten up to on the second floor of a church.

"If Mitch were here," Jimmy said, "he'd remind you how sad you two make Jesus."

Megan laughed. "My dad used to say that any time I had a boy over. Even if it was just to study."

"Well, if you all must know, we didn't do anything," Billy said. "I mainly comforted and consoled her."

"And I mainly just cried," Sarah added, letting out a slight laugh to relieve any remaining tension.

Billy placed his hand on her thigh and she covered his hand with hers. "We hashed some stuff out."

"So, you're both good now?" I asked.

"We're not exactly going to date, but we're closer than friends," Sarah informed us.

"So, what does that mean exactly?" asked Jimmy. "Are you on the market again?" He raised a solitary eyebrow on his forehead and stared longingly at Sarah.

"You wish," Sarah said with a laugh.

"We're just going to remain close friends," Billy said.

"Friends is good," Melody chimed in. She sat up in the seat, stretched her slim arms over her head, and yawned. Then she turned her head to her right and stared right at Billy, her smile growing twice its normal size.

Her first crush was back on the market, and her pre-adolescent plans of landing Billy Bardem as her boyfriend were very much back on the cards.

Billy turned to his left and looked at her, doing a double take due to how disturbing her maniacal grin was. A grin she held as her smoldering eyes drilled into him with unrelenting infatuation.

"And if you see us holding hands, or doing anything else that you might consider romantic, just go with the flow. That's what we're doing. So, don't hold us to any expectations. These are strange times, and so don't expect normal from us." Sarah looked at Mel too, who was still grinning at Billy with all her teeth.

Leaning forward in his seat, Billy whispered just behind my ear. "Is she all right?"

I glanced over my shoulder at my little sis, and solemnly shook my head. "Not since she was born, I'm afraid."

"Hey," Melody protested. "I heard that!" She gave the back of the seat a kick and Sif sat up to see what was going on.

"I have an announcement too," Megan said, glancing periodically into the rearview mirror, but making sure to keep one eye on the road. We all turned and looked at her. "I love you guys."

"Ah," Sarah said, reaching up from the back seat and giving Meg's shoulder a firm squeeze. "We love you too, Powerhouse."

"No," Megan said, shaking her head. Her bright blue eyes flashed in the mirror once more. "You don't understand, Long Legs. I really, really love you."

"And I love you… You big goof."

Sarah practically climbed over the front seat and hugged Megan. Her arms still wrapped around Megs, Billy, Jimmy, Mel and I shot curious glances back and forth to one another.

"Uh… Long Legs?" I asked.

"Yeah," Megan said. "That's her nickname."

Sarah fell back and plopped down in her seat beside Billy again. She rolled her eyes.

"Sarah 'Long Legs' Lewis?" Jimmy asked.

"It's dumb, I know," Sarah answered.

"No," Melody said. "It's not dumb. It's fitting. Even I want legs like those, someday."

"Why thank you," Sarah replied, grabbing the hemline of her short skirt and doing a mock curtsy, even though she was seated.

"Guys… quiet!" I said, raising my hand. "Megs, slow down, and pull over up here." I pointed at a spot on the side of the road and she pulled the Mercedes over, its tires crunching on gravel as we came to a full stop.

Not waiting for anyone to figure out what I was going on about, I reached over Jimmy's waist and opened the door. He leaned back as I clambered out. To everyone's confusion, I climbed onto the hood of the car so I could get a better view, and stared out at ultra-violet glowing creatures moving steadily across the highway about half a mile away.

Megs opened the driver's door and stood, resting her arm on the window and looked up at me and then peered out into the distance to try to see whatever it was I was looking at.

"What do you see, Travis?"

I pointed into the darkness. "Over there."

Megs gave up trying to see from her position and climbed up on the hood of the car with me, the hood barely managing to hold our combined body weight.

"They travel in herds," I said.

Megs nodded. "That's so awesome."

By now everyone had climbed out of the car to

see what it is we were looking at. In the distance, half a mile down the road, a massive heard of at least forty or more aliens like Lucy crossed the highway.

"I guess we just wait here for a while and let them pass," Billy said.

"I just hope they stay over there," Jimmy said.

"As long as we keep our distance," Sarah said, "I think we'll be fine."

Everyone nodded in agreement and, huddling together as we leaned against the car, we watched the marvelous migration of these strange creatures from another world in quiet wonder.

6

DOWNFALL

PART 6: CODE SILVER

CODE SILVER WAS HOSPITAL PARLANCE which meant someone had brought an unlawful firearm into the building. Me and Mel's mom had always told us, if you ever see a gun in a public place and you get scared or feel like the person might be a threat, you yell "Code Silver!" and then get to safety.

As gunfire erupted, we all flinched and watched the herd of aliens scatter. The familiar rumble of the V8 rode up on them, causing the aliens to panic and stampede. The man in denim and Vinny rode in back of the truck while a third guy drove. They fired off their M60 machine guns as they chased down some of the aliens that broke off from the larger group.

The aliens whined and squawked, sounding like how I'd imagine dinosaurs would sound, as they fled for their lives. Bullets pelted the side of one of the creatures and it went down. That's when its partner flared its tails and, tips glowing bright pink, it cut through the front wheel and axel of the truck.

Metal screeched and the truck's left front tire broke off and the vehicle did a nose-dive. Skidding to a stop in the field, the two men in back were thrown from the bed of the truck and tumbled to the ground.

They immediately pushed themselves up, but Vinny wasn't fast enough to raise his gun in time, and the angry alien pounced on him and began to maul him with the ferocity of a rabid bear.

The denim man swapped out the ammunition belt of his fully-automatic M60 for a fresh one and turned all of his firepower onto the monster as it gored his friend to death.

The beast wailed in agony as the man in blue denim burned through the entire hundred rounds of his ammunition belt, riddling it with lethal bullets. Staggering to the side, the creature let out a sad sounding moan, as it bled a bluish-turquoise blood from its multifarious wounds. We could tell it was in pain.

It squawked one last time, as if calling out for help, then collapsed to the ground as it finally went down.

"Yeah!" The man cheered. "That's what I'm talking about!" He rested his machine gun on his hip, holding it tight as its barrel glowed orange hot in the dark morning hours. At the same time, he pumped his other fist victoriously.

By now, the driver stepped out of the truck, and drew out his own M60, proving he was armed just as heavily as his hunting buddies. He fired off a couple of warning shots at two of the beasts that were circling back to check on their mates. Catching the hint, the aliens paused, snorted and huffed, and reluctantly turned back the way they'd come.

"That's right," the driver shouted. "You git-outta-here, you Earth invading, resource-stealing, ugly bunch of stinkin' aliens! This is our planet! So, you git!" the driver shouted. He then aimed his gun at the herd, which was already in full retreat, and fired off some shots just for the heck of it.

The two surviving men whooped and hollered and fired additional victory shots into the air. Even though they'd lost one of their own, it seemed of little consequence to them. After all, by their reckoning, they were at war. All that mattered was winning. And they had two more kills on their belt and, for them, that was the important thing.

"They're killing them!" Melody gasped, watching with abject horror as the slaughter unfolded before her eyes. "We need to do something!"

"I wish we could, kiddo," Sarah replied. "But it's safer for us if we don't get tangled up in all of that."

"Right now," Billy said, adding his own two cents, "I think the best course is to avoid any big towns and try to make it to Maple Park. We'll camp there for tonight."

"Why spend another night out here in the wild," Jimmy asked. "We have enough gas to get to the city."

"But we don't know if it's safe," Sarah answered.

"She's right," Billy affirmed. "If we set up camp in Maple Park, one or two of us can scout the city in the morning, check to see if it's safe, and come back and tell the others."

"That's a good plan," I said, agreeing with everything that had been discussed so far. "But what if we run into more yahoos like them?" I jutted a thumb over my shoulder in the direction of our gun-toting highwaymen.

"Sticks and clubs aren't much against guns," Melody said. "We need more firepower."

"Agreed," Jimmy said.

"I don't know," I said, looking back out at the hunting party. "Maybe stealth would be best."

"Avoiding any unnecessary contact with those idiots is to be desired," Megan said. "But Jimmy and your sister ain't wrong, Travis. If we do have a run in, things could end badly for us if we don't have a means to properly defend ourselves."

"More guns?" I asked.

"More guns," Billy stated.

I thought a few seconds more on it and then nodded. "Billy, you're the only one with any real training, so I think you should be the one to carry it."

Megan put her fist to her mouth and cleared her throat. I was about to say something more when she did it again, this time slightly louder and with more urgency. We all looked at her.

"I'm the four time, women's elite stage, close-range shooting champion," Megan informed us.

Both of my eyebrows practically raised to the top of my forehead. "You're what now?"

"I thought you knew me, Travis. All those trophies on my shelves. What did you think they were?"

"Roller derby trophies," I replied.

"Well, yeah, sure. Some of them. But I've only been doing roller derby for two years. We don't have that many bouts per year."

"So, what you're saying is, you have more than a dozen trophies for shooting?"

Megan nodded. "Yeah. Is that such a surprise?"

"No, I mean… yeah, sort of. But that's beside the point. Why are you carrying around a hockey stick instead of a gun?"

"I like to bash idiot's heads in. It's much more satisfying to hear the crunch of their skulls as they cave in."

"You're kidding me, right?"

Megan looked at me, her face serious. She shrugged. "What? You knew that about me."

"You're morbid," Melody said, squinting at Megan. Then, a wide smile broke across her face. "I like it!"

We all laughed. "I told you, Megs is a Powerhouse," Sarah said. "Nobody bad-talks her, because they know that they'll get folded up like a lawn chair and stuffed in the garbage."

"Well, that's where garbage people belong," I said,

looking at Megs and smiling.

"Very true," she said, flashing me a smile of her own. She brushed a tuft of blonde hair out of her eyes and blinked at me, her blue eyes sparkling in dawn's early light.

Jimmy pulled out his map and slammed it down on the hood of the car. "There's a fairly large town between us and Maple Park called DeKalb."

"DeKalb?" Melody asked. "That's its name?"

"That's what the map says," replied Jimmy.

We all shrugged off the strange name, since most towns in America either had traditional sounding names like Springfield, Shelby, and Maple Park, or it had weird sounding names like Tarnov, Nebraska, Ding Dong, Texas, and Dekalb, Illinois. Heck, there was even a town called Santa Claus down in Indiana. But none of that was neither here nor there.

"There should be a pawnshop or something there," Sarah said. "Something that sells weapons, at least."

Billy pressed his finger down on the map, singling out Dekalb. "Then, that's where we're headed."

We all piled into the silver Mercedes, and Megan

drove us into DeKalb. As we approached the city limits, she flicked off the headlights and we drove up and down the streets during the civil twilight hours of early dawn looking for a gun and ammunition store.

Eventually we ran across a pawn shop called 'Zemeckis's Pawn Shop' and Megan pulled the car around back, to help keep us out of view.

The back door was locked, but Jimmy made quick work of that by finding a cinder block and using it to bust out the back door window.

Glass shattered and tinkled to the ground. We looked around and nonchalantly stepped inside just as the sun was coming up and highlighting all the houses in predawn pink hues.

We were like kids in a candy store at Christmas. Megan and Billy looked over the pistols while Sarah tried out the various bows and crossbows. She eventually settled on a bright red Martin Archery, Pro-series *Firecat* bow.

Melody found a couple of large kukri knives that had a cross halter so she could sheath double blades across her back.

Jimmy found himself a pump-action shotgun, flash-grenades, and one World War II claymore which we made him put back. As much as Jimmy was our unofficial explosive expert, we couldn't risk such a device going off and taking all of us along with it.

He replaced it with a bandolier replete with heavy penetrating slugs and even put on a red head band so as to look like his favorite movie hero, John Rambo.

"Jed, eat your heart out. I'm going full Rambo," he announced. He chuckled at his good fortune and cocked his shotgun.

"Jed?" asked Melody. "Who's that?"

"It's Patrick Swayze's character in the film *Red Dawn*," I informed her.

"Oh," she said, going back to looking at knives. "I don't really care for war movies."

"Best two movies ever made,!" stated Jimmy with full confidence. "And this, right here," he added, pointing at all the stuff in the store, "is our *Red Dawn* moment."

Jimmy wasn't wrong. We were just kids, but when it came down to it, we would defend each other with our lives.

Continuing with the task at hand, I found a classic bolt-action, Winchester model 70 hunting rifle with top-mounted scope and .308 caliber bullets.

Once we were armed to the teeth, we headed outside. The sun was finally up and the town felt tranquil. We loaded all our stuff into the trunk of the Mercedes, which still had room for all the weapons and camping gear. Then we piled in, and Sarah taking over for Megan, drove the rest of the way to Maple Park.

Unfortunately, when we got to Maple Park, most of it was burnt to the ground. Like our town of Woodridge, it had been bombed to smithereens. Even the hospital was mostly demolished and the fire station was burned to ash.

"Over there," Jimmy said, pointing toward a patch of green grass outside. "The baseball park."

"What about it?" I asked.

"We can set up our tents there. It's in the middle of town, the bleachers and retaining walls will block the wind and maybe even the light of our campfire.

"Good thinking," Billy said. He looked over at Sarah, who nodded, and turned the wheel as we pulled into the parking lot next to the field.

She parked the car between the chain-link fences and some pine trees, to help hide our position, and we all got out and spent the next forty-five minutes setting up camp.

Once we had four tents set up around a campfire, which we placed in front of the pitcher's mound, we dragged over a couple of benches from the dugout and got out the cast iron skillet, a couple cans of Hormel chili, some Spam, and a bag of saltine crackers. It wasn't exactly a gourmet cookout, but it was better than nothing.

Starved out of our minds, we ate in complete silence—all but for the clanking of our spoons on our metal dishware. The clanking had an almost rhythmic quality to it and I helped myself to a second bowl of chili, but instead of keeping it for myself I set it down on the ground beside me and let Sif have something to eat too.

Sif snarfed down the entire bowl in record time and began licking her chops, making loud smacking noises as she did. This struck us as funny, and we all masked giggles and snorts, trying our best not to laugh at the dog who was just doing what dogs do.

"So, I have to ask," Jimmy said, still chewing a mouth full of beans, "what are tonight's sleeping arrangements? I mean, we have four tents and there's six of us. I'm fine sleeping alone, but if we need to pair up, I'm fine with that too."

Mel raised her hand. "Billy and I will share a tent."

Sarah laughed and grabbed Mel's wrist and drew down her hand. "No, little lady. You and I will be sharing a tent."

"Fine," Mel said, letting out a disappointed sigh.

"I'm fine sharing a tent with Travis," Megan said. "That will leave a tent for you and Billy," she added, looking over at Jimmy.

"Works for me," Jimmy said, taking another spoonful of chili.

"Good," I said. "It's settled then."

Jimmy pointed his spoon at Megan and I and, flecks of chili falling out as he spoke, said, "You two don't do anything I wouldn't do… because there's a lot I could think of that I would do if I had a girlfriend as hot as Megan."

Megan leaned forward as if she were going to get up off the bench and go over and clobber Jimmy, but I grabbed her arm and pulled her back down to her seat and prevented any unnecessary beatings.

"We're not there yet," I informed everyone. "But I thank you for your consideration about my super-hot girlfriend and my love life."

"Thank you, babe, for saying I'm super-hot."

"The facts are the facts," I retorted.

Megs grabbed me around the neck and pulled me into her. We all sat and watched the fire for a while, letting a nice calm settle over us.

After brief yet peaceful quiet, Melody finally broke the silence. "Do you think it's true what Dr. Castle said about you being infected with alien DNA?" she asked, looking over at Sarah. "Do you think it's killing you?"

Sarah gazed into the flames of the fire, her face growing serious as she gave the question genuine consideration.

"I don't know. I mean, I don't think so. All I know is that I feel fine. And if it was destroying me from the inside out, you'd think there'd be signs."

"I think it was just a lie," Billy said, stirring the fire with a stick. "A way for him to justify pumping her full of his miracle cure when, in actuality, all he was doing was poisoning people."

As Billy churned the ash and charcoal, Jimmy grabbed some more branches from the pile we'd gathered and threw them onto the flames. The dry branches mixed with brown pine needles crackled and popped, and spat up a flurry of sparks that flashed hot-orange and then quickly dissipated.

"I think Billy is probably right," Megan said, reaching over and touching Sarah's knee. "But if anything starts to feel out of the ordinary, you let us know, okay?"

"I will." Sarah smiled and pressed her hand onto Megan's, which rested on her knee. Megs gave her a squeeze and then sat back and leaned against me.

Melody snapped her fingers and sprang up, "I just remembered," she said, spinning around and running to her bag. She promptly unzipped it, rummaged through her things, then pulled out a plastic bag of Jet-Puffed marshmallows. Racing back to the fireside, she held up the bag and said, "I found these in the kitchen cabinet in the dining hall at the science lab."

"You're a genius!" Jimmy said, jumping up and grabbing a couple of branches. He whipped out a knife he'd gotten from the pawn shop and began carving the stick into a smooth skewer. He made three of them and passed them around. Billy had a long two-pronged fork which he used to roast his mallows with.

Megs and I shared a stick while Melody and Sarah shared one too. Jimmy kept the third stick for himself and we all roasted marshmallows by the fire.

"So good," Melody said, peeling off the crisp golden skin of the mallow and stuffing it in her mouth, its gooey insides remaining on the stick.

"Hot, hot, hot," Jimmy yelped, having shoved a freshly roasted marshmallow into his mouth. He chewed with his mouth open to help dissipate the heat and we all laughed.

Eventually, after having had our fill of marshmallows, Billy was the first to head to his tent and go to bed. Then Melody. Followed by Jimmy shortly thereafter. Finally, Megs and I parted ways, giving Sarah silent hugs before leaving. When we ultimately climbed into our tent, she was sitting by herself, staring at the fire, lost in thought.

Before I zipped up our tent, I looked at Sarah one last time and wondered what she might be thinking. With everything that had happened to her, from her getting poisoned and nearly killed, to the whole ordeal with Billy, and the drama of having been attacked by one of the aliens, I couldn't imagine any of us taking it as well as she seemed to be doing. She wasn't even crying. Just staring, deep in contemplation, into the dancing flames.

"Good night, Long Legs," I said. Sarah laughed and looked over her shoulder at me. "Good night Maverick. Sweet dreams."

"You too," I said, and then finished zipping the tent. When I turned around, Megan was lying on our sleeping bags and patted the area next to her, beckoning me to come cuddle.

We snuggled up together and effortlessly fell into a deep sleep. I didn't stir till morning and would have likely overslept if it hadn't been for Megan calling my name.

"Travis!"

"Huh?" 'I mumbled, still half asleep.

"Travis, get up." She was insistent and her voice sounded a little panicked.

"What is it?" I yawned and stretched and slowly crawled out of the tent. Standing up, I rubbed my eyes to find Megan standing at the foot of Sarah's tent. She pulled back the flap.

"She's gone."

"What?" I asked, yawning again. "Who's gone?"

"Sarah. Your sister. Billy. Jimmy. All of them." Megan marched across to Billy and Jimmy's tents and opened them up too. "They're all gone."

At a loss for words, we stood staring at each other, neither of us knowing what to say.

7

DOWNFALL
PART 7: MELODY "MAYHEM" MAHONEY

"People don't just disappear into thin air," Megan said, pacing back and forth in front of the still smoldering campfire. "At least, not our people. They wouldn't have just left without saying anything. Something happened to them. I'll bet my life on it."

I nodded. There wasn't much I could say because her concerns were my concerns too. But, whoever took them in the night made two big mistakes. One, they kidnapped Billy "Backwoods" Bardem, and I could already see three signs he'd left behind to help us track wherever it was they were taking them.

The second mistake was taking my sister Melody, the most defiant twelve-year old girl on this side of the planet. Obstinate wouldn't even begin to describe her.

"Over here," I said, pointing at one of the

branches in the pine tree.

"A broken branch?" Megan asked.

"Yeah," I replied. "It's a sign from Billy."

"How do you know?"

"See how it's broken and just hangs pointing down? A broken branch with the break on the left means they went west." I walked a couple of trees over and found another broken branch. "Another branch, this time the break is on the right."

"Let me guess," Megan mused. "A break on the right points toward the east?"

"Bingo," I replied.

We both looked to the right. The highway was the only thing to the south-east. Nearing the main road, I pointed out the third thing. A trail of sand and gravel that curved south-east.

In all likelihood, Billy would have bent down and grabbed a handful of dirt as they were being taken and left a trail to show which way the vehicle turned onto the highway as they pulled away.

"And this sand line," I added, pointing down at the trail of sand, "turns in that direction." I traced the trail with my finger and raised my hand so that I was pointing east and we both stared down the road.

The trail of sand pointed in the same direction we had just come from yesterday. Which likely meant the militia red-necks from earlier tracked us down in the night and nabbed everyone they could carry.

"It seems they took them back that way," I said, pointing up the highway.

"It was probably those alien-poaching jockstrap-for-brains we saw earlier."

"That'd be my guess too," I said.

Megan ran to the car, dropped the keys down from the visor and caught them in her hand. Then, she put them in the ignition and tried starting the car. But, to our frustration, the ignition didn't turn over or make any noise but for a single mechanical clunk.

We looked at each other and, determined to find our friends, she tried again. But the car was deader than dead. When she twisted the keys a third time the steering column locked up and the keys got stuck in the ignition.

"Pop the hood," I said. She did as asked and I ran around to the front of the car and raised the hood. Inside were severed wires which had obviously been cut and a missing battery which they had taken, ensuring we wouldn't be using the car again anytime soon. "Well, crap."

"What did you find?" asked Megs, getting out of the car.

"They took the battery and cut the wires making sure we couldn't put a new one in."

"Those assholes," she said, drawing up beside me and taking a look for herself.

I shot her a worried look then ran to the back. As I suspected, the trunk had been jimmied. When I touched it, it sprang open on its own only to reveal a whole lot of nothing. "They took our weapons too."

"Hey, you kids looking for your friends?" a voice rang out. It was so unexpected that Megs and I were completely caught off guard.

Startled so badly we jolted with fright, we quickly spun around to find an old man with gray hair, hoary three A.M. stubble on his creased and weathered face staring at us. He leaned against a walker as he stood across the street from us and waited patiently for our response.

"Oh, hello," I said.

"Where did he come from?" Megan asked in a hushed voice. I shrugged.

"Did you see where they took them?" I asked.

"Our friends, I mean."

"Sure did," he replied, pointing up the road. "To the old meat packing plant. They've been taking the bodies of the aliens there. But, this morning, I saw them drive off with your friends."

"How deep asleep were we?" I asked.

Megan shook her head and pinched the bridge of her nose and thought. "Crap," she said.

"Crap?" I asked.

"As in, oh, crap. I think we were drugged."

"The marshmallows!" I exclaimed.

"Dr. Castle must have dosed those as well."

The old man had started hobbling back up the street when Megan called out to him. "Hey, mister. Do you know where we can find some wheels?"

"As a matter of fact," he replied in a feeble old man's voice, "I do."

He pointed down one of the main streets at one of the few building still standing. The police station. And parked outside was a squad car.

"Keys should be inside a key cubby on the wall next to the dispatchers desk in the main office."

"That's very specific," I said. "Did you work there?"

"I was the Sherrif here for twenty-three years. I retired last year due to my bum hip." He nodded down at his walker, emphasizing his point. "But with everyone run outa town, there's nobody here but for those who were disabled and couldn't keep pace."

"I'm sorry," Megan said.

"No, it's quite all right. I'm old. I've lived a full life. It doesn't matter what happens to me. But you kids have your whole lives ahead of you. So, you go save your friends from that bunch of yahoos."

"Yes, sir," I said, saluting. The old man saluted me back, even though I could practically hear Megans eyes rolling in her head.

Sure enough, the keys were right where the old man had said. What's more, there was an entire armory that one of the keys on the rack unlocked. We managed to get two shotguns, one long rifle, a Baretta 92F semi-automatic, and a Rueger Security-six revolver from the gun rack.

As Megan and I packed up the gear, I couldn't help but feel Jimmy was right when he said it was a *Red Dawn* moment. As a group of young boys, that was our favorite movie. We saw ourselves in the young teens of Calumet who were forced to defend their town from Soviet invaders. Swap out the Russians for aliens and, well, you have our story. More or less. *Go Wolverines!*

Megan drove as I loaded and checked ammunition. As we headed out of town, we could see the old meat-packing plant. It was an industrial sized complex with numerous tin buildings, lots of piping, and old unhitched semi-trailers everywhere.

"If they see a squad car pull up, they might open fire. We should sneak around to that building over there where all those pickup trucks are parked," I said. "Start are search for everyone there."

Sure enough, once we'd hidden the squad car so that it was out of sight, we ducked low and crept around to the other side of the building. That's when we found the burgundy Chevy pickup truck, the same one we'd crossed paths with earlier, backed up to one of the loading bays.

"Up there," Megan pointed. I looked up to see what she was pointing at. It was an open window two stories up, and was cracked open just enough that we could easily pry it the rest of the way open and slip inside.

The only problem, I thought, was that there was

nothing up there but a solitary pipe. A pipe that we'd literally need to crawl across to get to the window.

"We can get up over here and then shimmy across," she said, pointing at the dumpster in the back that gave access to an overhang that would let us get onto the ledge with the pipe.

"It looks risky," I said. "But, right now, I don't see another way in. At least, not one where we could slip in undetected."

So, agreeing this was our best option of gaining access to the facility, we climbed up the dumpster and side of the building and then scaled the pipe. Halfway across the pipe, my foot slipped and I almost toppled off the ledge if it wasn't for Megan's quick reflexes. She caught me by the collar of my jacket and hoisted me up and set me back down onto the pipe all in one fluid motion.

"Exactly how strong are you?" I asked. "Like, on a scale of Wonder Woman to She-Hulk."

"Neither," she said. "I'm She-Ra level strong."

"Dang," I said. "Out-nerded by a girl."

"In my household, there's no such things as nerds, or geeks, or dweebs. Just people with eclectic interests."

"I like that," I said. "So, you do roller derby, shoot guns, and like animation. What else should I know about you, Megs?"

Our backs flat against the serrated steel wall of the building, she looked over at me and smiled. "Just that my favorite movie is *Pretty in Pink* but I also really love that new *Back to the Future* movie."

"You saw *Back to the Future*?" I asked, growing excited. She was a woman after my own heart. Because, in my opinion, it was one of the best movies ever made—certainly the best time-travel movie to date.

"Like, three times."

"Like, for real?"

"Why would I lie about watching one of the greatest sci-fi films of all time?"

"I guess you wouldn't," I said with a shrug.

"Maybe I just like it so much because I have such an epic crush on Michael J. Fox," she said, looking at me from the corner of her eye to gauge my reaction.

"You like him?" I asked.

"Of course," she said. "He's super cute," she informed me, letting out a kittenish laugh. Reaching back, she placed her hand on my chest and added, "But

I think you're much cuter, Travis Mahoney."

She winked at me and then turned back around and cautiously took her first step out onto the pipe.

We shuffled along the pipe until we got to the window and, as Megan pulled the window out, she looked back at me, and asked, "You ready for this?"

"Ready as I'll ever be, I guess."

She brushed a blonde tuft of her hair back behind her ear, smiled again, and reached out her hand to help me up and over the windowsill. I took her hand and climbed in through the window and then turned around and helped her through too.

Once we were inside, we found ourselves on a catwalk high above a large facility with crates, cattle guards to corral the animals, and different tools spread all about the entire shop area.

That's when we heard the sound of a power saw. It didn't sound all that friendly, and our optimism was suddenly weighed down by our overwhelming concern for our friends.

"Did you hear that?" I asked.

"Let go of me, you dumb-ugly-meat heads!!!" a small voice screamed.

"I definitely heard *that*," Megs said.

"Melody," we stated at the same time, recognizing my sister's precocious way of speaking.

We followed the sound of Mel's berating, as she let her kidnappers have a big ole helping of her profanity-laced two cents.

"The mouth on that girl," Megan said.

I sighed. "I know, right? Maybe her nickname should be Melody 'Mayhem' Mahoney."

"I like the sound of it," Megan said, pursing her lips and nodding in agreement.

"You touch me there again, you bald, egg-headed, mustached weirdo, and I'll scream. I swear to God, I'll..."

Suddenly, her voice turned muffled, even though she didn't stop cursing at the top of her little lungs. We followed her suppressed screams until we found her. Looking down from the catwalk, we saw Mel tied to a chair, her mouth gagged with a rag. She wriggled and squirmed, trying her best to break free, but her bonds were too tight for her to escape.

"Where are the rest of them?" I whispered.

"Beats me," Megs whispered back. "But let's focus on rescuing your sister first. Then, after she's secure, we'll find the others."

I nodded and she looked over at a coil of rope that sat on the catwalk nearby.

"Hand me that, will you?"

I did as asked, and she tied the rope to the railing and then waited for the guard, who'd tied Melody up, to leave. She dropped the rope down and then, swinging one leg over the railing then the other, she climbed down.

Megan dropped the last five feet and landed with a padded thump. I quickly scurried down the rope behind her and almost fell onto her head, missing her by an inch. Although, I didn't stick my landing and fell flat on my ass.

Masking my embarrassment, I immediately sprang back to my feet, dusted my butt off, and said, "I meant to do that."

Megs gave me a crooked grin and then raced over to Melody and untied her. I then reached over and pulled her gag down and her mouth promptly started up again.

"What took you so long, you big idiot? And who sleeps through a kidnapping anyway? My big dumb, useless brother… that's who."

I quickly replaced the gag, putting it back on her mouth, and made sure it was secured. As you might expect, this didn't go over very well with Melody, and she started yelling even angrier muted profanities at me.

"It's better this way," I said, looking at Megan who replied with an aptly timed eye-roll.

"Where are the others?" asked Megan. Melody was still too busy screaming at me to hear the question, so Megan grabbed Mel's shoulders and gave her a firm jerk as she forced my sister to turn her whole body toward her, along with her attention. "Where are the others?" Megan repeated.

She pulled down Mel's gag and then waited for her to answer.

"They took Billy and Jimmy and threw them in the back of some kind of meat freezer. They're probably icicles by now. I don't know what they did with Sarah. But it was strange. She wasn't tied up. She was just sort of casually talking to them."

"Talking to them?" I asked.

"Maybe you need to have your ears checked," Melody quipped. "Because that's what I just said."

"I heard you fine," I answered. "I was just confirming what you were saying. We have only one chance to pull this rescue off, so I wanted to be sure. Is that all right with you, your Highness?"

"I guess," Melody said out of the corner of her mouth, letting out a reluctant huff to go along with it.

"Here's what we're going to do," Megan said. "You two go find the boys, and I'll go hunt down Long Legs."

I watched Megan slink away, keeping low as to stay out of sight, and I kicked myself for not grabbing her and kissing her. Or, at the very least, wishing her good luck.

"She'll be fine, lover-boy," Mel remarked, then she let the ropes around her wrists unravel, fall to the ground, and she reached up and took me by the hand. "This way."

We wove through several rooms before we came to the back and found a row of walk-in freezers. Mel pointed at the second door from the right and said, "That one. They're in there."

I went and opened it and found Billy and Jimmy sitting on a cardboard box of frozen steaks, rubbing their arms and shivering. They looked over at me, frost adorning their eyebrows and hair.

His teeth chattering, Jimmy said, "Boy, are we glad to see you, Trav."

Melody raced inside, shoved Jimmy out of her

way, and helped Billy up. "Don't worry," she said, taking his arm and tossing it across her tiny shoulders. "I've got you."

"Gee, thanks," Jimmy sarcastically quipped, his teeth still clacking as he shivered. "Just discard me like garbage, why not?"

"Come on, you guys," I whispered, waving them along. "Stop diddle-daddling. We've got to go find Sarah and Megan."

"Why? Where's Megan?" asked Jimmy as he stepped out of the freezer.

"She went to get Sarah," Mel replied, answering his question for me.

"Yeah, what she said."

"If only we had our gear." Jimmy scratched his chin, thinking how best to go about rescuing our girls. That's when I had a brilliant idea.

I whispered into Jimmy's ears and then pulled the police keys out of my pocket and slapped them into his hands. His face lit up and he replied, "I'm on it!"

With that, Jimmy ran to the nearest exit, poked his head out, and when he deemed the coast was clear, he exited the building.

"What in the world did you say to him?" asked

Mel. She gave me a probing look, one of her eyebrows rising on her forehead with curiosity.

"You'll see," I said.

"Hey, you kids. What are you doing out?" a man's voice shouted.

We looked over to find the man in blue denim marching toward us. As he drew closer, he paused and looked at us. "Wait just a darn minute. You're new. Where's that other kid? The ginger one with all the freckles?"

Mel reached over and gripped my hand so tightly I thought my bones would snap. But I squeezed back, reassuring her that it would be all right.

"He, uh, he had to, um… pee," I replied.

"Yeah, yeah," Billy added. "He was about to piss himself. So, one of the guards came and got him."

"Which guard?" the denim man asked.

We looked at each other and realizing we weren't getting anywhere, I pulled out the Glock 92F and tossed it to Jimmy while I drew up the revolver.

Turning toward the man with guns raised, we both started firing off warning shots. Bullets pinged and ricochetted all over the machinery in the room and the man in denim jumped out of the way and ducked behind one of the meat slicers.

"Run!" I shouted as I shoved Melody toward the exit. She quickly ran to the back doors and slammed into the crash-bar and flew outside. Billy and I slowly backed off, firing intermittently as we crept toward the door.

"You kids realize we have your girlfriends, right? Both of them," the man said. "You just going to take off and abandon them?"

He took his cowboy had off of his head and raised it above the machine, waving it in the air. We both stopped shooting and the lull in hot-leaded rain coerced him to come out from behind his hiding place.

Raising both hands in the air, the denim man said, "I'm not armed. I just want to talk."

"And I want a Whopper from Burger King right now," I said, "but we don't always get what we want."

"Very funny, kid. But this is serious. Do you know what we'll do to your little girlfriends if you leave them here with us?"

"Yeah," Billy said, "absolutely not a damn thing. Ask me how I know?"

"How do you know?" the man asked.

"Yeah," I said, turning toward my best friend.

"How do you know?"

"Because," he replied, a grin spreading wide across Billy's face. "That alien you caught before you separated us. The one trapped in the cage that's in the same room where our girls are right now…"

"Yeah, what of it?" the man in denim asked.

"He's with us."

"Lucy is here?" I asked. Billy nodded.

"What are you kids going on about? Who's Lucy?"

"Lucy is our… alien," I said.

"You named it Lucy?"

"No, you dipshit," I said, raising my gun. "My little sister did."

I fired a warning shot, and as the bullet whizzed by his ear, forcing him to duck, Billy and I dashed out the back door.

"Is Lucy really here?" I asked.

"Yes," he said as we ran toward the neighboring building. "We all saw him in a cage when we arrived. He must have followed our scent, and then got caught by these hunters. Sarah went to see if he was all right."

"Sarah did?" I asked. "But doesn't she hate Lucy?"

"She hates would-be rapists more. That a-hole in

the hat was sniffing your little sisters hair when they took her away. We had no idea where they'd taken her. Sarah made a deal with them so that she could get close to Lucy and let him out. Lucy is our ticket out of here."

"What kind of deal?" I looked at Billy who slowed to a stop. We stood out in the open, his face clouding over with a grim look that didn't exactly thrill me.

"That doesn't matter now," he answered. "What matters is, she's now going to be held hostage unless we go back and break her out."

"Oh, I'm already three steps ahead of you, my friend."

Billy shot me a perplexed look. "You are?"

That's when we heard the sirens wailing and, shooting past the side of the building, was Jimmy "Mad Dog" Polson, driving recklessly and doing donuts in the parking lot as he acted as a distraction.

"Go, Mad Dog!" I shouted, throwing my fist up in the air.

Jimmy reached out the open driver's side window and raised his fist and replied with a hearty, "Woo-hoo!"

"As for my sister," I said, turning around. "She

shares a telepathic link with Lucy, and they should be… arriving right… about… now."

Right on time, Lucy burst out of the glass windows at the other end of the building and landed on the ground. He shook off any shards and ran up to my sister who emerged from behind the dumpster that Megs and I had passed on our way in.

Nuzzling each other and touching their foreheads together, Lucy stretched out in front of Melody and let Mel climb onto his back.

At the same time, we heard another eruption of gunfire, and the back door flew open and Megan held Sarah around her waist with one arm. In her other arm, she held up a pump-action shotgun and fired off a shot. BLAM!

"Somebody help me with her!" Megan shouted between blasts of her gun.

Billy ran up and scooped Sarah into his arms. "What did they do to her?"

Megan loaded more slugs into the chamber of the shotgun as she spoke, cocked it. "They drugged her," she informed us. "They had her tied to a bed in the main office. I don't think anything happened, but I did shoot three assholes in their groins on the way out here."

"Nice," I said.

Megan held up a finger. "Just one sec," she said. Then, looking like the friggin' Terminator, she started walking toward the back door and fired round after round at it, pumping it full of slugs.

BLAM! BLAM! BLAM!

Finally, after depleting all her rounds, she opened the door and the denim man stumbled out. Holding his gut, he collapsed to his knees. His chest and abdomen were full of holes. Bleeding out, he looked up at Megan with a shocked expression on his face.

"Pedophiles like you don't deserve to live," she sneered. Flipping her gun around in her hands, she cracked the denim man in the side of his skull with the butt of her gun and he went out like a light. With a thud, his body hit the ground and Megan simply turned her head to the side and spat in disgust.

Lucy and Melody skidded to a halt beside us and Billy hoisted Sarah onto Lucy's back. "Get her out of here," he said. "Meet us back at the baseball park."

Melody nodded and with that, they raced off.

The moment they left the complex, two trucks came skidding around the corner. Both vehicles came up alongside Jimmy's patrol car and boxed him in.

As the two pickups wedged him in, one of the men drew a rifle and aimed it at Jimmy through the open car window. To their dismay, however, Jimmy merely grabbed the barrel, used it to hoist himself out of the car, leaped into the back of the pickup bed, and then with one more leap, jumped out of the back of the truck.

Jimmy hit the ground and rolled several times before looking up, dust falling from his hair. Surprisingly, his red headband had stayed on the entire time, and he reached up with an arm and gave me the thumbs up.

"You know that claymore we told Jimmy he couldn't have," I asked.

"Yeah," Billy replied as his eyes fell to the remote detonator in my hand.

"Well, he kept it," I said. I flicked up the red tab and then hit the switch. The two trucks, along with the squad car, went up in a huge ball of flame.

Jimmy, although a safe distance away from the explosion, covered the back of his head with his arms and stayed down as rocks and debris rained down all around him.

"Holy smokes!" Billy said, sinking low to the ground.

"Go Renegades!" I shouted, throwing my fist up again.

Both Jimmy and Megan raised their fists into the air too, and shouted, "Renegades!" at the same time.

Billy did a double take, looking at all of us with a pleasantly surprised look on his face.

"Who are you people?"

"We're the mother-effin' Renegades of Summer, man," I told him, cad smile forming on my lips. "That's who."

8

DOWNFALL
PART 8: RENEGADES OF SUMMER

ONCE WE HAD RETURNED TO THE BASEBALL field, our de facto base camp, we gathered around the cheerleader, Sarah Lewis. She was the girl of the hour, the girl who kept looking out for us. If Billy Bardem was the glue that held our group together, Sarah was the backbone. She was our protector and our nurturer. Which is why we were all so worried about her not waking up.

Having returned to the baseball diamond, we tried to process the trauma of the past several hours. For a bunch a kids who never asked to have to survive an alien invasion, or have to fight off dangerous humans such as rogue soldiers, mad scientists, and self-appointed militia extremists, it was a lot.

Megan sat on her knees and held Sarah on her lap

and in her arms as she stroked her blonde hair. "Come on, babe," Megan said, "you've gotta wake up."

"What did they give her?" I asked.

Megan shrugged. "I don't know. But it seems like she's been roofied."

Jimmy looked at Sarah's face and then, reaching down, lifted her eyelids and checked her pupils. Her eyes were most definitely dilated.

"Whatever they gave her," he said, "it's strong. Her pupils are dilated and she's completely out of it."

"Will she be all right?" Melody asked. She stood behind Megan and looked over her shoulder at Sarah's peaceful resting face.

"She strong," Billy said. "She'll weather this like she has every other terrible thing that's happened to her in the past week."

"I'm surprised they didn't drug me too," Mel said.

"You're too small," Megan said. "If they would have given you something, it would have stopped your heart and you'd be dead now."

"Oh," she said solemnly, realizing she'd been further into the jaws of the lion than she'd understood and was, without even realizing it, in a battle for her very life. She grew extremely silent and just stared out into the distance for a while, doing her best not to cry.

Noticing the sudden worry that came over Melody's face, Megan felt instant regret for being so blunt.

"Sorry," Megan said, apologizing to Mel for her straightforwardness. "That came out wrong. It wasn't my intention to scare you."

"It's all right," Melody replied, pressing her hand down onto Meg's shoulder. Megan reached up and touched Mel's hand and turned her head and smiled at her. "We're living in scary times."

"True that," Jimmy said, nodding in agreement with Mel's statement. He reached up and tightened his red headband, securing it so that it wouldn't slip down over his eyes.

"I'll stay by her side until she's through this," Megan said, still stroking Sarah's hair. "The rest of you, try to get some sleep. We should be fine here tonight with Lucy guarding us. But there's no telling how many more of those militia nuts are out there, so we best not stick around too long."

We all looked over at Lucy, who merely sat off to the side, panting like a domesticated dog.

"Speaking of guard dogs," I said. "Where'd Sif go?"

"She took off when the bad men came," Melody answered.

Megan moved Sarah over to their tent, gently set her down, and climbed in with her. Before she zipped up the tent for the night, she looked at us all one last time and said, "See you all in the morning."

"You bet," I replied.

"I don't think I can sleep," Jimmy said, holding up his hand. His hand wobbled in the air. "I'm still shaking from the adrenaline."

"Me either," I said.

"That makes three of us," Billy stated. We all looked toward Mel, who let out a big yawn.

"Not me," she said. "I think I'll go to bed now, too. I'm pooped." She slowly got up and trudged languidly over to her tent, dragging her feet as she went.

As her brother, I could tell she was putting on a brave face and trying to act mature, like always, but was secretly scared. After everything that had happened to her today, no one could blame her.

"Goodnight, sis," I said. I smiled affectionately at her and she stuck her tongue out at me and then climbed into her sleeping bag and hit the hay.

Melody began snoring the moment her little head

touched her pillow. Meanwhile, Billy, Jimmy, and I sat by the fireside staring vacantly into the flames.

"Hey, do we have any more of the marshmallows?" asked Jimmy.

Billy and I looked at him in disbelief and, at the exact same time, shouted, "No!"

"What'd I say?" he asked.

"It was the marshmallows from the lab that drugged everyone and allowed those goons to kidnap you all in the first place," I informed him.

"Oh," he said, with a shrug. "I just thought we were so exhausted we couldn't move."

"This incident has set us back a couple of days," Billy said. He looked back up at us, his dark brown eyes flitting from mine then to Jimmy's. "Tomorrow, a few of us need to head into the city and scout things. See how bad it is there."

"I'll do it," I said. They both looked at me. "I'll take Melody and Lucy with me," I added.

"Safety in numbers," Jimmy said. "Smart."

"Safety with an alien," Billy replied.

"Precisely," I said. "We'll look to see how bad the damage is and see if the government evacuated the city like they have all the other towns along the highway."

"Just be careful," Billy added. His voice grew direly serious. "For all we know, the aliens did a number on the city too. Not to mention, looters and runaway mobs most likely have done some serious damage as well."

"We will," I affirmed.

It wasn't long until our adrenaline had worn off and we began to feel the effects of weariness overcome us. Jimmy was the first to grab his sleeping bag and set it beside the fire. Billy and I copied him and we all went to sleep listening to the gentle crackle and occasional pop of the burning logs.

Sometime during the middle of the night, I heard strange breathing and cracked open my eyes to find Lucy standing directly over me. I was nervous but not scared and waited to see what he was going to do.

"Uh, hey there, boy," I said, trying not to sound afraid. "Can I, um, help you with something?"

Lucy didn't move aggressively and his breathing was calm, so I was able to relax a bit. Randomly, Lucy craned his neck forward and pressed his forehead against mine, like a cat would their owner.

"Um… okay," I said. It felt weird, but I rolled with it. A couple of seconds later I felt a weird energy, kind of like a plasma ball that sends all the electricity to your fingertips when you touch it. The kind you find at novelty shops.

Next, I saw flashes of images in my mind. The flashes turned into full on visions and it felt as though I was teleported back to the meat packing plant.

In the vision, I saw myself standing over the denim man who still laid on his side, slowly bleeding out. As I stood over him, I heard a sharp whine, like that of an animal, and turned to my right to see what it might be. To my surprise, it was Sif. She was standing there next to the man, panting. It seemed as though she might know him.

I watched Sif lick the man's face, rousing him from the brink of death. Although he had one foot in the grave, there was enough life left in him for him to sit up.

The vision blurred, momentarily, and then Sif's happy golden retriever face disappeared, leaving only darkness. But I couldn't help but feel something was there, lingering in the darkness, just beyond my eyesight.

I tried to mouth the words "Hello" but nothing came out. That's when I realized this was more of a memory than a live broadcast. Maybe twenty feet from where Sif had stood, there was a dark figure wearing a cloak. It manifested itself, stepping into the light of the lamp that flickered periodically above the rear exit.

Whoever it was, though, they just stood there, watching the man in denim. It was as if they were some kind of ghostly specter waiting to ferry the dying man across the River Styx to Hades, where he would suffer eternal torment for his evil deeds in this life.

Finally, the figure walked over to the man, crouched down beside him, and in a low, soft voice, whispered, "The kids that were here today. Which way did they go?"

"Why would I tell you?" the denim man grumbled. He coughed up a blotch of blood-laced phlegm and spat it onto the ground next to the mysterious person in black.

The hooded figure looked down at the spittle by their foot and then looked up again, but didn't respond to the rude gesture. They didn't need to. It was clear he wasn't here for the man. The denim man meant nothing to him.

Not uttering a single word, the dark figure merely

reached into the man's wounds with their fingers. He pushed them all the way into the denim man's gut, up to their last knuckle and forced an unbearable groan from the man's pale lips.

"Those kid's asses belong to me. To me, do you hear me? So, you can just go to Hell."

The dark figure didn't speak, but merely twisted their fingers inside his gut, stretching and tearing the already damaged tissue. The denim man screamed out in agony and coughed up more blood before the hooded figure paused their torment.

"I'm only going to ask you this one more time. Which direction did they go," they demanded.

The dark figure's voice was calm but to the point. Again, it was clear that the denim man was just a stepping stone on their way to them finding us, and they were perfectly fine torturing the man to get the information they needed.

"The baseball diamond," the denim man replied, finally having had enough. "The baseball diamond in town."

The figure patted the man on the head. "Now, was that so hard?"

"What do you want with those damned

troublemakers anyway?" the man groaned, clutching his bleeding gut.

The black figure stood up, drew out a sword, twirled it around so that its blade flashed in the moonlight and raised it high above their head.

The denim man threw out his hand and pleaded with the dark figure. "No, wait, I can help you. I can—"

Before the man could beg for mercy, the figure brought the blade down onto his skull. The sword went through his head, entering the top and coming out beneath his chin.

Fresh blood trickled down his already crimson stained lips and jaw and his wide-eyes stared vacantly out at nothing as he rapidly faded away. As if the man didn't matter, the dark figure slowly rose back to their feet, dislodged the sword from the man's skull, and wiped the blood off the blade using their sleeve.

I leaned forward and tried to peer under the hood of the cloaked figure when, sensing somebody watching them, they spun around to face me.

I jumped back in fright as we came face-to-face, our eyes locked onto one another. In that moment of terror, I didn't know if they could see me or not. I staggered back, afraid they might have seen me, but my concerns abated when they asked, "Who's there?"

Obviously, I couldn't answer them. But it was interesting that Lucy's telepathic powers enhanced my mind so much that another mind was able to sense it.

Without warning, I woke up from the vision and shot up in bed. Gasping for air, my entire body was drenched with sweat and it felt as though I'd just awaken from a terrible nightmare.

"What on God's green planet Earth was that?" I asked, still a little shaken from this psychic event. My chest heaved and my lungs burned as I took in another gasp of cool night air.

Lucy, finished with whatever it was he was trying to show me, trotted off to the side of Mel's tent and gave me space to gather myself. Curling up next to my sister's tent, Lucy laid down and closed his eyes.

Amazing, I thought. Lucy had warned me of a potential threat and let me know that someone was looking for us. But who were they? And why did they want to find us specifically? Naturally, I was left with more questions than I had answers for.

Just then, I heard the zipper of one of the tents open and Megan stepped out of her tent.

She had on only her gray cotton panties and a

tight-fitting white tank top that was partially see-through.

"What's the matter, Trav?" she asked, shooting me a worried look. "You screamed out in your sleep."

I shook my head. "You know how Melody always says that Lucy is telepathic?"

"Yeah." Megan tossed a few branches onto the fire, to keep it going, and then sat down next to me, crossing her legs crisscross applesauce. She rubbed my back soothingly. "I remember her saying that."

"Well," I said, "I think she might be right."

Megan looked over at Lucy, who was now fast asleep, and asked, "Did it try to talk to you?"

"It gave me a vision… I think."

"A vision of what?"

"The denim man. He wasn't dead yet. And then Sif found him. And, in my dream, Sif isn't alone. There's a dark hooded figure following her."

"Then what happens?"

"The figure tortures the denim man a little bit and he dies. It's all kind of vague. Like a dream you can barely remember after waking up."

"That's it?"

"Yeah. I'm afraid so."

"Why would he show you that?" Megan rubbed her chin as she thought on it some more. Then, flopping onto her back, she stretched herself out on my sleeping bag as she laid down next to me.

"Beats me," I said. "Maybe he was warning us about the person in black? I don't know. I can't remember the details, but it feels like they were looking for us. But that's all I got before I snapped out of the trance."

"That's not much to go on," Megan said.

"Maybe it'll come back to me."

Megan's skin looked golden delicious in the fire light and she laid back on my sleeping bag, her arms folded behind her head, her tank top riding up to expose her stomach.

"Travis," Megan asked, after a long pause.

"Yeah?" I replied. "What's up?"

"What are your thoughts on marriage?"

I gulped. That was the most unexpected question I'd ever received. It's not that I hadn't thought about it, but we were both too young for marriage. At least, I felt so anyway.

"Uh, I, um..." I stammered, not knowing how to respond to that. "I guess I, uh... well, you know."

She didn't take offense by my indecisiveness, but merely stared and me with her piercing blue eyes and patiently waited for me to come up with something.

I tugged on the collar of my shirt, as it had become restrictive all of a sudden, and it felt like it was choking me. "Of course, I do want to get married someday."

"Would you want to marry me?" she asked. Her baby-blue eyes still held my gaze, and I didn't dare look away for fear of offending her.

"Uh.. yeah. I mean, sure. I'd be honored."

She looked back up at the sky and let out a drawn out, almost disappointed yet deliberate sigh.

"I'm sorry," I said. "I don't know what you want me to say."

She laughed. "I don't want you to say anything. I only ask that you be honest with me and tell me the truth, no matter what."

"Even if it might hurt you?" I asked.

She continued to gaze up at the stars and simply nodded in response to my question. "Yep. Even if it might hurt me."

"Well," I said, drawing out the pause to tease her with anticipation of what I'd say next. "There is one thing I feel you should know."

"What is it?" she asked, looking right at me with an almost alarmed sort of look. Her voice definitely sounded worried. "Tell me."

"You fart in your sleep, just like your brother."

"I do not!" she practically screamed, her eyes growing wide with shock. She laughed and then reached over and pinched my arm.

"Ouch! Don't kill the messenger," I squeaked.

"Oh, I think the messenger lies," she replied.

Resting my hand on Megan's hip, I leaned across her chest and looked her straight in the eyes. "The messenger would never lie to the woman he loves."

"Will you two just stop that lovey-dovey crap and have sex already!"

We looked up to see Jimmy lying on his side, leaning on his elbow, hand propping up his head as he stared at us from across the fire.

"Ignore him," I said, gently reaching down and, with the soft touch of my fingers, guiding Megan's chin back toward me. Once our eyes realigned, I brushed her beautiful face with the back of my hand and smiled at her.

We kissed by the firelight, Jimmy watching us

with bated breath, hoping it might turn into something more. As we kissed, Megan reached up and silently flipped Jimmy the bird.

"Very mature," he said sarcastically.

When Megan finally got up and returned to her tent, she walked the short twelve or fifteen steps swiveling and swaying her hips like a runway model. Naturally, this tease was meant to gratify me and torture Jimmy.

"In ten years from now, when you two are on your tenth kid, don't' complain to me about the sleepless nights. My god man, you're the luckiest son-of-a-B that I know."

"Go to sleep, Jimmy," I said.

"Yeah, go to sleep, dick-wad. You're keeping everyone awake," Melody said from her tent.

That sparked a round of laughter and I was a little embarrassed to discover everyone was still wide awake and had been politely listening in on our conversation the whole time.

"Fine," Jimmy replied. "See you all in the morning." Then, right on brand, Jimmy lifted his leg and let one of the loudest, wettest, nastiest farts any of us had ever heard rip. It ripped so hard, we thought it would tear the very fabric of space-time, if not the fabric of his shorts.

"Dude, you might want to change your pants," I said. "Seriously."

"I'm good," Jimmy said, flashing me his classic 'Mad-Dog' grin.

As exhaustion slowly won out over me, I looked over at Megan's tent. She'd left the flap open and was sitting next to Sarah, who slept peacefully. Megan noticed me staring at her and she smiled, made a heart symbol over her left breast, and then blew me a kiss. I smiled, and then, let my consciousness drift off to sleep.

DOWNFALL
EPILOGUE

WHITE SMOKE ROSE INTO THE AIR AS BILLY, Jimmy, and I doused the fire in the special way that only boys are capable of doing. Melody stepped out of her tent to find us all putting the fire out together and she quickly cried out, "Ew, gross."

Megan and Sarah emerged from their tents in time to watch us finish peeing on the pile of smoldering ashes as we put out the fire. They stood in silence and watched us and, among the five of us, there was no embarrassment, no reaction, just full on acceptance. My sister was the only one who seemed to be disturbed by us killing two birds with one stone—that is to say, putting out the fire and taking care of business.

"Don't be mad," I said, shaking the last few drops out. "It's a camping tradition."

"It's an idiotic boy tradition," Melody countered.

We finished doing what needed to be done and tucked everything back in and went over to help the girls pack up the tents and camping gear. Lucy, meanwhile, stretched out like a cat, front paws forward, yawned, and then laid back down.

As we packed up our gear, Melody broke out a Hershey's chocolate bar and fed it to Lucy who seemed eager for his treat.

"We're out of food," Billy said. "We'll have to scavenge up some more."

"In that case," Sarah said, "maybe we should all head into town together." She sounded a lot better now that the drugs had worn off and she'd had some proper rest.

"Sarah's not wrong," Megan said. "I'd feel a whole lot safer if we stuck together. Especially after Travis's vision."

"Vision?" asked Jimmy. "What vision?"

"I'll tell you guys later," I said.

"I'm sure we'll find something to eat the closer we get to the city," Billy added. "Until then, we'll have to tough it out."

It wasn't long before we finished loading up the Mercedes and got back on the road. As we headed out of town, we passed a white Lutheran church with a white spire. Jimmy, who sat on my right in the front passenger seat, pointed it out and said, "Hey, you guys, maybe we should pull over so you two can get married."

Megan, her hands on the wheel as she drove, slowly turned her head and glared at Jimmy. "Do you want to walk the rest of the way to Chicago, smartass?" she asked him.

He shook his head, no, and laughed. "Sorry. Didn't know it was such a sensitive subject."

Everyone rode in silence for the next forty miles or so and, we must have looked silly too, because our trunk was open with a giant alien sitting in the back.

"Do you think Lucy is cold?" asked Melody. She looked back and peered under the decklid of the trunk at her pet alien.

"I honestly don't know," Billy said, turning around and looking out the back along with Melody. "But seeing as how their skin doesn't like how bright our daylight is, I'd assume they prefer the cold and darkness. I mean, he seems to do better at night than in the day."

Melody nodded and then, turning around in her

seat, she grew excited and pointed out the window. "Hey, guys, look at that."

She pointed at a road sign on the side of the road that read: Chicago fifteen miles.

Like her, a wave of relief came over us. We were almost there. The trip had taken five days, but we were finally coming to the final leg of our journey.

"Pull over here," I said, pointing at a Circle K gas station by the side of the road. Nobody was around and there were no cars, so it seemed safe.

We parked the car next to the pumps and Billy got out and put the pump in. To our amazement, the pump still worked. In fact, the closer we got to the city the more it seemed things worked. The lights worked. The radio worked—even though it mainly just played the emergency broadcast system's warning messages on repeat. Even the gas pumps were operational.

The only weird part was the complete lack of people. But we all assumed they were evacuated like the majority of our town. Still, we had to keep a lookout for unfriendly aliens and people alike.

As the car filled up with gas, we went into the station to look for things to eat and maybe perhaps use the bathroom if they had one.

"You stay here, Lucy," Mel said, touching Lucy's forehead and, perhaps, communicating telepathically with her alien companion.

"Holy lucky clovers," Jimmy exclaimed, as we entered the convenience store. "This place has everything!"

We each grabbed arm-baskets and began filling them up with everything from beef jerky to sunflower seeds, to Twinkies. Jimmy even filled an entirely separate shopping basket full of cans of his favorite soda, Pepsi-Cola.

The girls grabbed additional items like toothbrushes, Band-Aids, rubbing alcohol, cotton wipes, bottles of spring water, and some feminine products.

By the time we'd shopped to our heart's content, the store shelves were half barren. Our supplies replenished, we sat outside under the shade of the gas station fueling canopy and leaned against the gas pumps as we had ourselves a feast of gas station snacks and fizzy sodas.

Jimmy belched and then said, "Hey, Trav, pass me another pop, will you?"

"Yeah, no problem," I said, and I tossed him

another Pepsi. "Here, catch!"

He snatched it out of the air one-handed, pulled the tab, and cracked it open. The can hissed and Jimmy threw back his head and gulped it down in record time. Tossing the emptied can aside, he let out a contented sigh and then burped even louder than before

"Did anyone ever tell you that you're gross?" my sister asked, glaring disapprovingly at Jimmy and his crude antics. Her glare was hard and menacing and would have been ten-times scarier if she wasn't a small kid.

"Did anyone ever tell you that you're overly opinionated?" he fired back. Just for good measure, he willed out another burp and blew it in her general direction. Melody held up her hand as a barrier and turned her face away.

Billy and I snacked on beef jerky while the girls split a deli sandwich they'd found in the refrigerator.

"Does it seem strange to anyone else," my sister asked, "that the electricity is still working the closer we get to the city?"

"Not really," Sarah replied. "Illinois has six nuclear power plants. More than any other state in America.

They should be able to power the whole of the state even in emergency situations like this."

"That's probably why they flew mom and the other patients from the hospital to the city. They knew it would still have power, even during a crisis event."

"That's why we're going to find your mom," Megan said. She wasn't trying to feed me false hope, but, rather, sounded genuinely confident. "She's here. She has to be," she continued. "I can feel it in my bones."

"In that case," I said, standing up. "Let's get this show on the road."

Everyone nodded and we packed up all of our things and piled back into the car. As we pulled out of the gas station, we turned onto the main road headed to the Windy City. Before we'd even traveled fifty feet, however, Megan slammed on the breaks, sending us all lurching forward.

Jimmy, who wasn't buckled up, slammed forward and smacked his head on the dash. Rebounding off, he fell back into his seat.

"What the Hell, Megs?" he said, rubbing the knot that was already forming on his forehead.

The rest of us grew deathly silent when we looked out the windshield to see what it was that had caused Megan to abruptly hit the brakes.

Standing in the center of the road, with Sif standing next to them, was the person from my vision. The black cloaked figure.

"It's them," I said.

"Them who?" Jimmy asked, still rubbing his head.

"The person from my vision," I replied.

Everyone gulped nervously and looked back out at the cloaked figure blocking our path.

"What do you think they want?" Mel whispered.

"I don't know," I said. "But I have a feeling we're about to find out."

Reaching behind their back, the mysterious figure drew out a samurai sword, pointed it at us, and said, "Get out of the car."

"Well, that puts a damper on things," Billy said.

"What do we do?" Melody asked nervously.

We heard a loud clunk above us and jumped in fright as Lucy climbed onto the roof of the car. Lucy squawked like a velociraptor and pawed at the rooftop, her claws scraping the paint right off the metal. It sounded like nails on a chalkboard, but a hundred times worse.

In response to Lucy protecting us, the figure in black took an offensive stance. Sif's hair stood up on her back as she lowered her head and began growling a deep, intimidating growl.

"Well, this isn't good," I said.

We all shared concerned looks as we tried to figure out what our next move would be. It was then that Megan glanced back at everyone and said, "Stay here. I've got an idea."

Without waiting for any of us to ask what she was planning, she got out of the car and slowly walked toward the person in black.

"Brilliant idea," Jimmy said in his most facetious tone. "Walk up to the person wielding sharp pointy things. If she gets stabbed, I suggest we all run and don't look back."

"We're not leaving Megan," I said.

"That's because you're whipped," Jimmy said, snapping his fingers at me.

"Be serious," Megan whispered. "Now isn't the time."

Jimmy nodded and we turned toward the intense encounter continuing out our windshield. Megan raised her hands in surrender, inching forward slowly one foot at a time. "We don't mean you any harm," she said.

The dark figure lowered their blade and, in a commanding tone, ordered Sif to "Heel." Being the good dog she was, Sif stopped growling and dutifully sat down beside their master.

Megan took a few more cautious steps toward the mysterious figure, who merely sheathed their sword. Megan paused and looked back at us and then looked forward again in time to see the mysterious stranger slowly reach up and draw back the hood of their cloak.

"Long time, no see, Powerhouse," the figure said, addressing Megan by her roller derby nickname.

Beneath the shroud was a beautiful, dark haired Asian girl roughly the same age as Megan and Sarah. When she raised her face and blinked her brown almond shape eyes, Megan covered her mouth and smothered an audible gasp.

"Jen?" she asked, still confused by the encounter. "Is that really you?"

"Yes," Jen laughed. "It's really me."

"Hot damn," Jimmy whispered as an aside to himself, although we all heard it. "I don't care who she is, but she's like ten-million on the Scoville scale."

"That's pretty hot," I said.

"Yeah," Jimmy swooned. "I'm in love."

Sarah Lewis sat forward in her seat, and with a shocked expression plastered across her face, she gasped, "I don't believe it."

"Believe what?" asked Billy.

"It's Jennifer Nakamura," Sarah reiterated. "She was with us at Make-Out point when Lucy..." Sarah paused and looked over at Melody with apologetic eyes. "When Lucy killed all my friends."

"How is she alive?" I asked. "How did she survive the Massacre at Make-Out Point?"

"I guess I never saw her get killed," Sarah said. "I mean, I saw Lucy chase Jen into the woods and, I suppose I just assumed the worst. I assumed nobody else had survived."

By the time we'd built up the nerve to get out of the car, Megan and Jennifer Nakamura were already hugging. Tears of relief and joy trailed down their cheeks and they laughed, grateful to be reunited.

Sarah stepped forward, her mouth hanging open in disbelief, and timidly asked, "Jen?"

Jennifer Nakamura looked over at Sarah Lewis,

and, in that moment of recognition, said, "Hey, there, Long Legs. You're looking as hot as ever."

Sarah laughed and then ran into Jen's open arms. Rushing into one another's embrace, Sarah and Jen practically fell over hugging. Megan shrugged and threw herself onto them, adding them to the dog pile. They all laughed and cried and rejoiced in the unexpectedness of this reunion.

"What I wouldn't give to be the meat in that three-girl sandwich," Jimmy shared, letting out a sigh of pent up longing.

"Don't be a perv," my sister chastised.

Once Megan, Sarah, and Jen had their fill of tears and hugs, they slowly rose back up and dusted themselves off and turned toward the rest of us.

Jen looked over at Lucy and asked, "Is that thing safe?"

Melody stepped in front of the car, throwing out her arms and protecting Lucy. "He's my friend," Melody said. "He protects me and I protect him."

"Interesting," Jen replied.

Sif ran up to me and I knelt down and scratched her behind her ears. "We missed you, girl."

Sif let out a gentle bark and I laughed.

"If you plan on staying with us," Billy said, walking up to Jen, "Just know we're headed into the city." He turned toward the Chicago skyline and we all looked out at the vast cityscape that sat on the horizon.

"That would be a bad idea," Jen informed.

"Why?" asked Jimmy. "Why's that a bad idea?"

"Because," Jen said, turning back toward all of us. "The city is where the hive is."

"The hive?" I asked.

"The aliens are laying eggs," she replied. "And they're fiercely protective of their territory. If you go in there and take one wrong step, you're not coming back out alive."

"But we have Lucy," my sister said. "He'll help us get through the city safely." We turned toward Melody who reached out and placed her little hand upon Lucy's forehead. "He'll help us get mom back, won't you, big guy?"

Lucy huffed, not so unlike a horse, and gently swayed his head. Melody's face lit up and she threw her little body against Lucy's giant head, wrapped her arms around him, and gave him the best bear-hug she could muster.

"He said, yes," she chirped. "He's going to help us

rescue mom."

"That's good enough for me," Billy said.

We all nodded and Jen Nakamura turned toward us and scanned all of our faces as she tried to decide what her best course of action was going to be, given the circumstances.

After giving it some thought, she took a deep breath and slowly exhaled. "You people are crazy." We gazed at her, knowing that this couldn't be her final answer. Sure enough, a couple of seconds later, a devious grin gradually crept onto her lips and, her eyes narrowing, she said, "Count me in."

TO BE CONTINUED IN:

THE LORDS OF SUMMER REBELLION

ABOUT THE AUTHOR

Tristan Vick is a multi-genre author specializing in science fiction, fantasy, and horror, and has also dabbled in mystery and suspense. He graduated from Montana State University with degrees in English Literature and Asian Cultural Studies and speaks fluent Japanese. He lives with his wife and three children in Japan. When he's not commuting on the train or teaching English, he spends his time reading, writing, binge-watching his favorite television shows, and eating sara-udon. In addition to being traditionally published, Tristan Vick continues to self-publish under his imprint, Regolith Publications, LLC, and Regolith Comics. His comic book series, The Astonishing Adventures of Alicia Carter & Robot, has sold over 10,000 copies in its first year of release. His other comic book works include Daughter of Wolves, The Profane, Blood & Chrome, The Viking Berserker Zarna, and Animal Woman.

ALSO BY TRISTAN VICK

▼ Available Now ▼

The Resurrection Saga
BITTEN: Resurrection
BITTEN 2: Land of the Rising Dead
BITTEN 3: Kingdom of the Living Dead

The Valandra Time Cycle
Valandra: The Winds of Time (Book 1)
Valandra: The Dragon Blade (Book 2)
Valandra: The Goddess of War (Book 3)

The Chronicles of Jegra:
Gladiatrix of the Galaxy (Book 1)
Imperatrix of the Galaxy (Book 2)
Destroyer of Galaxies (Book 3)
Galaxy Under Siege (Book 4)
Galaxy at War (Book 5)
A Song for the Galaxy (Book 6)

▼ Other Books ▼

The Profane (Novelization)
The Lords of Summer 1986
The Lords of Summer Invasion

Visit Tristan Vick's author website at:

www.tristanvick.com